Newcastle

City Council

Newcastle Libraries and Information Service

☎ 0191 277 4100

...ase return this item to any of Newcastle's Libraries by th
...hown above. If not requested by another customer the l
be renewed, you can do this by phone, post or in per
Charges may be made for late returns.

"Jessica."

He exhaled the word as if he'd been waiting a lifetime to say it. In a way he had.

Ryan was pleased he'd never asked her for a photograph. It couldn't have glimpsed upon the reality of her features. Hair the colour of drizzled sand was tucked behind her ears, eyes the shade of the richest dark chocolate peeked out beneath dark lashes. She smiled as if she was greeting her first date—nervous, expectant, unsure.

Worried. Just like he was.

After so many months of writing one another, meeting in person was kind of surreal.

"Jessica." When he said it this time it made him smile. "It's so good to meet you."

She grinned as he walked toward her, then opened her arms to him.

"Ryan."

Even the way she said his name did something to his insides, made him nervous, but he pushed past it. He was a soldier. He was trained to deal with difficult situations.

"I'm so glad you made it, Ryan."

He let the flowers drop to the porch as he opened his arms to hold her. Jessica stepped into his embrace, arms tight around him. Hugging him like someone who cared.

Like he hadn't been hugged in a long time.

Dear Reader

I have always been captivated by the idea of a couple falling in love before meeting one another. What could be more romantic than writing letters to a stranger and then anxiously waiting to meet that person in real life almost one year later?

When United States Army Ranger Ryan meets cancer survivor Jessica, the bond they've formed on paper instantly translates into real life. But their romance is not as simple as falling in love. Ryan has a past to confront and a son to reconnect with, and Jessica needs to battle her own demons from the past.

This is my second book about a soldier returning from active duty, and it certainly won't be my last. There is something special about a man in uniform coming home with a wall around his heart and finding a woman to open him up and tame him.

I hope you enjoy this heart-warming story, and don't forget to visit me at www.sorayalane.blogspot.com

Soraya Lane

THE
ARMY RANGER'S
RETURN

BY
SORAYA LANE

First published in Great Britain 2011
by Mills & Boon, an imprint of Harlequin (UK) Limited,
Eton House, 18-24 Paradise Road, Richmond, Surrey TW9 1SR

© Soraya Lane 201

ISBN: 978 0 263 2:

Harlequin (UK) policy is to use papers that are natural, renewable and recyclable products and made from wood grown in sustainable forests. The logging and manufacturing process conform to the legal environmental regulations of the country of origin.

Printed and bound in Great Britain
by CPI Antony Rowe, Chippenham, Wiltshire

Writing romance for Harlequin Mills & Boon is truly a dream come true for **Soraya Lane**. An avid book reader and writer since her childhood, Soraya describes becoming a published author as 'the best job in the world', and hopes to be writing heart-warming, emotional romances for many years to come.

Soraya lives with her own real-life hero on a small farm in New Zealand, surrounded by animals and with an office overlooking a field where their horses graze.

Visit Soraya at www.sorayalane.blogspot.com

For Hamish, my husband and real-life hero.
You have always believed in me, and in my writing,
and this book is for you.

CHAPTER ONE

Dear Ryan,
It feels like we've been writing to one another
forever, but it's only been a year. When I say only,
a lot has happened in that time, but it makes our
friendship sound insignificant somehow.

Of course you can come to see me. It would be
weird not to meet you, after getting to know you
so well, but strange in the same way to put a face
to the name. When you are discharged, write to
me, or maybe we could use more modern forms of
communication once you're back in civilization.

Stay safe and I'll see you soon. It's unbeliev-
able that you could be back here and we'd pass
one another in the street without even knowing.
Jessica

JESSICA MITCHELL STARED out the window and started
pacing, eyes never leaving the road. She'd been like
this for almost an hour. Stupid, because it wasn't even
time for him to arrive yet, and he was army. He would
be exactly on time.

She knew that. Jessica knew he was punctual. She
knew he would be knocking on her door at twelve-noon
bang on.

She knew just about everything about him.

Ryan McAdams.

Up until now, he'd just been a name. A name that made her smile, that made her run to the mailbox every morning. But that's all it had been. Innocent letters, two people confiding in one another. Pen pals.

And yet here she was, pacing in her living room, waiting to meet the man in the flesh.

Jessica looked down and watched her hands shaking. They were quivering, her whole body was wired, and for what? He was her friend. Nothing more. A friend she'd never met before, but a friend nonetheless.

So why was she still walking obsessively up and down? She could just make a cup of coffee or read the paper. Take the dog for a walk and not worry if he had to wait on her doorstep for a few minutes.

Because she wanted this to be perfect. There was no use pretending. His letters had helped her through the last year, had stopped her from giving up when she could have hit rock bottom. And she wanted to say thank you to him in person.

The phone rang. Jessica pounced on it, her pulse thumping.

"Hello."

"Is he there yet?" her best friend asked.

Her heart stuttered then restarted again. She let out a breath. It wasn't him.

"Hi, Bella."

"I'm guessing the hunk hasn't arrived then."

Why had she ever told her friend about Ryan? Why couldn't she have kept it to herself? It was stupid even making a fuss like this. He was her *friend*.

"Jess?"

She flopped down onto the sofa.

"I'm a wreck. A nervous wreck," she admitted.

Bella laughed. "You'll be fine. Just remember to breathe, and if you don't phone me with an update I'm coming around to see him for myself."

"He could be overweight and unattractive."

Bella snorted down the line. Jess didn't even know why she'd said it. Since when did she even care what he looked like? Whatever he looked like didn't change the fact that his friendship had meant a lot to her this past year.

"Bella, I— Oh, my God."

She listened to the thump of footfalls on the porch. Heavy, solid men's feet that beat like a drum on timber.

"Jess? What's happening?" Bella squawked.

A knock echoed.

"He's here," she whispered. "He's *early.*"

"You'll be fine, okay? Put down the phone, close your eyes for a few seconds, then go to the door. Okay? Just say 'okay.'"

"Okay." Jessica thought her head might fall off she was nodding so hard.

She placed the phone down without saying goodbye.

He was here. Ryan was actually here.

Waiting outside her front door.

How could she know this man almost as intimately as she knew her best friend, yet be terrified of meeting him?

She looked at the letter on the table, reached for it, then tucked it into her jeans pocket. She didn't need to open it to know what it said. She remembered every word he'd ever written to her.

Jessica squared her shoulders and shook her head to

push away the fear. Ryan was here, waiting for her, and she had to be brave. It felt like she was about to meet a lover she was so nervous, but it made her feel queasy even thinking that way. One of her closest friends was standing at the door, and for some reason she was para- lyzed with fear.

Bella had gotten her all wound up in knots, and for what? She wasn't interested in meeting a man in *that* way, especially not now. And she didn't want Ryan to be anything more to her, no matter what he looked like. What she needed in her life were good friends, and he had proven that he was there for her when she needed someone.

Another knock made her jump.

This was it. There was nowhere she could go but forward, down the hall.

Unless she escaped out the back window...

A flash of brown streaked past her and she groaned. Hercules. She'd put him out the back with a bone and hoped he'd stay there, but he must have squeezed through the doggie door when he'd heard the knock.

At least he'd be a good distraction.

Ryan wondered if it were possible for fingers to sweat. His were curled around the paper-wrapped stems of a bunch of white roses, clenching and unclenching as he tried to figure out what to do with them. Out in front seemed too contrived, behind his back looked ridicu- lous and hanging at his sides just seemed more ridicu- lous, like he was trying too hard. Why flowers? Why had he felt the need to complicate things by bringing flowers?

He was going insane. He'd survived the trauma and heartache of years serving his country, and now a stupid

bunch of flowers was tying him in tight coils. He was
a United States Army Ranger. Practised, strong and
unflappable. He'd never have made the special ops unit
with nerves like this.

Clearly he was losing his touch.

Perhaps he should throw them into the garden? He
looked over his shoulder, beyond the porch, then listened
as the door clicked and a small dog started barking.

He was out of time. Ryan slowly, cautiously turned
back toward the house. He wanted to squeeze his eyes
shut, walk back down the steps and start all over.
Without the flowers dangling awkwardly from one hand,
and instead standing at ease on the doorstep in front of
her.

Ryan spun around as the door swished open.

"Jessica."

He exhaled the word as if he'd been waiting a lifetime
to say it. In a way he had.

Ryan was pleased he'd never asked her for a photograph. It couldn't have done justice to the reality of
her features. Hair the color of rain-drizzled sand was
tucked behind her ears, eyes the shade of the richest dark
chocolate peeked out beneath dark lashes. She smiled
like she was greeting her first date—nervously, expec-
tantly, unsurely.

Worried. Just like he was.

After so many months of writing one another, meeting in person was kind of surreal.

He went to move and something tiny hit him in the
knees and almost made him fall. By the time he looked
down a small dog was doing laps around his feet, before
disappearing back into the house with as much speed
as he'd arrived with.

Ryan laughed then looked back to the woman waiting to meet him.

"Jessica." When he said it this time it made him smile naturally, rather than feeling like a word-stuck teenager. "It's so good to finally meet you."

She grinned as he walked toward her, then opened her arms to him.

"Ryan."

Even the way she said his name did something to his insides, but he pushed past it. He was a soldier. He was trained to deal with difficult situations.

"I'm really glad you made it, Ryan."

He let the flowers drop to the porch as he opened his own arms to hold her. Jessica stepped into his embrace as if she'd been made to fit there, firm against his chest, arms tight around him. She hugged him like someone who cared about him.

Like he hadn't been hugged in a long time.

It had been years since his wife had died. Years since he'd felt the genuine embrace of a woman, one that wasn't out of pity, but out of something deeper, warmer.

Ryan inhaled the scent of her—the tease of perfume that reminded him of coconuts on a beach. The soft caress of her hair that fell against his neck as she tucked into him.

It felt good. No...even better than good. It felt *great*.

He cleared his throat and stepped back, not wanting to make her uncomfortable by keeping hold of her too long. Jessica leapt back from him like a bear from a nest of hornets, her face alternating between happy and concerned.

"I…"

"We…"

They both laughed.

"You first," he said.

Jessica grinned at him and rocked back and forth, arms crossed over her chest.

"I don't remember what I was going to say!"

Ryan shook his head and laughed. Laughed like he thought he'd forgotten how to, cheeks aching as he watched her do the same.

He bent to collect the fallen flowers.

"These are for you."

She blushed. When had he last seen a grown woman blush? It made a goofy smile play across his lips.

"Me?"

He nodded.

"It's been a long time since anyone gave me flowers."

Ryan watched as she dipped her nose down to inhale them, her eyes dancing along the white silhouette of each rose.

It had been a long time since he'd *given* a woman flowers.

"Do they give me passage inside?"

Jessica looked up at him with an expression he'd only seen once before. His wife had looked up at him like that from her hospital bed, full of hope, happiness shining from her face.

He clenched his jaw and stamped the memory away, refusing to go there. This was Jessica, the woman who had made an effort to write to him when most Americans seemed to forget what U.S. troops were facing overseas. This was not a time to dwell on the past.

"Yes." She looked sideways, away and then back, but he didn't miss the twinkle in her eyes. "Yes, it does. So long as you're prepared to meet Hercules properly."

"I take it Hercules is the small fur-ball who almost bowled me over."

Jessica reached out to Ryan and grinned. "Maybe if I'd given him a more insignificant name he wouldn't be quite so full of self-importance."

Ryan took the hand she offered and let himself be led inside. It felt too normal to touch his skin to hers, too casual, but when she looked over her shoulder at him and smiled, her fingers trailing away from his until she was just a woman walking ahead of him, he felt the loss of her touch like a limb had just been torn from his body.

The shock of doing normal things was something hard to get used to, after months being surrounded by other men in the desert. Each day started to merge with the next one…and home seemed like just a scene on a postcard.

Being back here wasn't something he had looked forward to, it was something he'd feared and wished he didn't have to confront again. But Jessica had been there for him, eagerly writing him back so he'd had something positive to concentrate on.

When everything else was gone, snatched away from him, Jessica had been there.

She'd come into his life when he'd been losing his way. When he'd almost felt as though his soul had been defeated, like he had lost his purpose. It was Jessica who had held each piece of him together when he could have lost hope.

Maybe she could help him now he was home, too.

Because nothing else had fallen into place since he'd returned.

A man could only hope.

Jessica set the flowers to rest in a vase on her bench and turned back to her guest.

"Shall we have lunch here or go out for something?"

Ryan shrugged. "I don't mind."

"But…?"

She laughed as he squinted at her.

"How did you know there was a *but?*" he asked.

Jessica tapped her nose. "You'd be surprised what I know about you."

Ryan flopped down on the sofa and crossed his legs at the ankle. He looked at home here, comfortable in *her* home. Aside from her brother, she wasn't used to seeing men in her space.

She didn't want it to bother her, but it did. Having a man around had become foreign to her. It felt too intimate, being so close, seeing him so…at ease.

Funny, she had expected being back in America to be hard for him, but it seemed like she was the one struggling.

"Okay, you got me." He gave her a smile that made her almost want to look away, but she didn't. The way his mouth curved, his eyes creasing gently at the corners, was exactly as she'd imagined he would look. Hoped he might look.

Her stomach twisted, as if her organs had been flipped then dropped. She wasn't meant to be thinking about him like that. Not now, not ever.

"The sun's shining, the ground is still wet from the rain last night and I'm desperate to be outside in the open. You've got no idea how good it feels—smells— outside here," he said.

Jessica beamed at him. She was still nervous, but the quiver in her belly felt as if it were less from worry than excitement. A day out with someone with whom she could just be herself was exactly what she needed.

Besides, it would be easier being around him on neutral territory. Even if he was just a friend, she wasn't ready to see a man in her house, on her sofa, like that. Not after Mark. Not after what she'd gone through this last year.

It sent a shiver down her spine just thinking about the last twelve months.

"Give me five minutes, I'll get my handbag and we'll go to the park."

"I'm guessing we have to take the mutt?" he teased.

Jessica cringed as she heard paws racing on the timber floor in the kitchen. Hercules was like a missile, as if he'd known exactly what they'd been talking about.

He sprung through the door and leapt onto Ryan's lap, tongue frantically searching out his victim's face.

"Hercules! No!"

Ryan grabbed him and held him at a safe distance.

"Five minutes?" He raised an eyebrow, ignoring the wriggling dog.

She nodded. "Sorry about him."

Ryan stood, eyeing Hercules. "I'll start the clock now."

She turned sedately and walked toward her bedroom as slowly as she could manage. She wanted to run, to sprint to her room and grab her things and not miss a moment of being in his company.

Ryan. His name was circling her mind over and over, like a record she couldn't turn off. Ryan.

He was everything she'd imagined he would be and more. When they'd first started writing, he was just a soldier. He was a man serving their country and she felt good giving support to him. But when they'd realized they had grown up within ten minutes of one another, something had started stirring within her. Then when he'd made noises of coming back home to California, to Thousand Oaks, she'd started wondering. That despite her insecurities, despite her worries about herself, she had a connection with this man. A man who understood her and wanted to meet her. But a man she only knew on paper, who wouldn't feel pity for her or treat her like an almost-broken doll because of what she'd been through.

And he was hardly a disappointment. In the flesh, he was even more commanding than he was on paper. Well over six feet and built like a man who could protect her on a dark stormy night in the meanest streets of Los Angeles. A man with dark cropped, slightly disheveled hair that begged to be touched, ice-blue eyes that seemed to pierce straight through her body. And beautiful lips that, despite all he'd seen and experienced, still hovered with the hint of a smile as he spoke.

Jessica scolded herself. Smiling over mental pictures of him while she was alone was exactly what she *didn't* need to be doing. Ever. Until she reached the five-year mark, until she knew she was in complete remission, men were strictly off her radar.

Jessica stole a quick glance at herself in the mirror as she passed and fought the urge to cross her arms over her chest. She was still self-conscious, but it was getting better. After all they'd said to one another, all they'd shared, she hadn't told Ryan. Couldn't tell him. Not yet. It was still too fresh for her, too raw, to share with anyone.

And she wanted him to just like her for herself. Treat her like she was normal and not a fragile baby bird in need of extra care.

She picked up her purse, squirted an extra spray of perfume to her wrist and reached for a sweater. She didn't know why, but today felt like a fresh opportunity, a new chance. She wasn't going to let her insecurities ruin it. Not when she had a man like Ryan waiting to spend the day with her.

Even if she was scared to death.

She utterly refused to let her past ruin her future. Not now, not after all she'd been through.

Today was about starting over.

CHAPTER TWO

Dear Jessica,
I've become desensitized to what we have to see
over here. I wait for my orders, I no longer cringe
when an explosion echoes around me, and I au-
tomatically squeeze the trigger to take down the
enemy. Does it make me a bad person that I no
longer feel? I'm starting to think I like being here
because it means I don't have to face reality. I
can pretend my wife didn't die and that my son
doesn't hate me. But I'll be coming home soon,
after all this time, and I'm not going to have any
more excuses.

Thanks for listening, Jessica. You don't know
how much it means to me to be able to write to
you, to be honest like this. I can't talk to anyone
else, but you're always here for me.
Ryan

"So how is it you've managed to stay away for so
long?"

Ryan shrugged and turned his body toward Jessica as
they walked. He made himself look away from Hercules
racing up and down the riverbank so he could give
Jessica his full attention.

"I guess I became good at saying yes, and the army were pleased to have me wherever I was needed."

"What about this time?"

Ryan chuckled. After so long being in the company of men, he wasn't used to the way a woman could just fire questions. So candidly wanting to know everything at once.

"What's so funny?" she asked.

Jessica was…what? Pouting? No, not pouting but she was definitely pursing her lips.

"You're very inquisitive, that's all."

She gave him a nudge in the side and rolled her eyes. Ryan tried not to come to a complete standstill, forced his feet to keep moving. He wasn't used to that, either. Someone touching him so casually, with such ease.

He'd definitely been away too long.

"I write to you for months, and you can't tell me where you are or why you're suddenly coming home on such short notice. So spill," she ordered.

He followed Jessica toward the edge of the lake, the water so still it looked like the cover of a postcard. The park was beautiful, much more attractive than he'd remembered it being, but after so long seeing sand and little else, everything about America seemed beautiful. The smell of fresh rain on grass, the softer rays of sunlight, not burning so hot against your skin that it made you sweat. Things you took for granted until they were snatched away.

"I can't tell you where we've been, you know that, but what I can say is that our last, ah, assignment was successful."

Jessica waited. He'd give her that. She could talk his ear off, but she knew when to stay quiet. Seemed to sense that he needed a moment.

"I'm a marksman, Jess." He paused and watched her, made sure she didn't look too alarmed. "I entered the special forces as an expert in my field, and it's why I've been deployed so long."

"But you didn't want to come home," she said softly. "What made you come back now?"

Ryan sighed and looked out at the water. It was so much easier just keeping this sort of stuff in his head. But he didn't have to tell her everything. It wasn't like he'd planned to come home, more like his hand had been forced.

If he'd had it his way he would have stayed away forever. That's what he *had* done until now. Now he was home and he had to deal with being a single dad for real. Not to mention the fact his son didn't want to know him.

He didn't like admitting something was impossible, but repairing that relationship could be like trying to bring someone back from the dead. It was his own fault, his own battle to deal with, and he'd been a coward to wait so long before confronting the problem.

But one thing he'd promised himself was that he was going to be honest with this woman. She'd done something generous for him, helped him from the other side of the world through her constant letters, and he owed it to her to be real and candid with her now.

"I had an injury a while back and it never healed quite right." He moved to sit down on the grass, needing to collapse. It was hard being so open, just talking, and he couldn't go back. Couldn't put into words what had happened to him then, that day he'd realized he wasn't invincible. "I've had a lot of pain in my arm, so I had surgery in Germany on my way back home, and the army wants me on rest until the physio gives me the all clear."

Ryan gritted his teeth and forced his eyes to stay open as his memory tried to claw its way back. The smell of gunpowder, the pain making his arm feel like it was on fire, and not being able to stop. Making his arm work, pushing through, pulling the trigger over and over until his body had finally let him down.

He clamped his jaw down hard and looked at Jessica. She was sitting, too, right beside him, legs tucked up under her as she stared at the water. As if she was the troubled one. He could see it on her face. That she was either reacting to his pain, or harboring her own.

"Jess?"

She turned empty eyes toward him, bottom lip caught between her teeth.

"That means you're going back at some point."

He raised a brow. Had she thought he was home for good? Had he made her think he was staying by something he'd said?

"Ah, all going well, I'll be deployed wherever they need me," he confirmed.

It was wonderful being back here in some ways, but it was also extremely difficult. He'd do his best, try to make amends, but he was a soldier. That's what he did. What he was good at.

She nodded, over and over again, too vigorously. "Of course, of course you're going back. I don't know why I thought you wouldn't be."

"I'll be here a couple months at least, then I have to figure out what to do. I'm eligible to be discharged, they've offered me teaching positions, but I'm just not ready to walk away from my men. I don't know where

I'll be deployed yet but it's my job to go wherever they need me."

Sad eyes greeted him when he looked back at her. She smiled, but he could tell something had upset her. He hoped it wasn't his fault. Seeing those bright eyes cloud over was not something he wanted to be held accountable for.

"What about your son?" she asked quietly.

Ryan sighed. His son. George. Now that was a topic he and Jess could talk about all day. Or maybe not talk about at all, as he'd been home a week already and they'd hardly spoken a word to one another.

"I don't know if I'm just not cut out to be a father, or whether he truly wishes I was back with the army."

He didn't say what else he wondered. That maybe his son wished he were dead.

Ryan picked up a stone and stood, then reached his arm back and threw it into the water. He'd meant to skim it, but instead the stone went a little distance then landed with a plop.

He shut his eyes and pushed away the anger. He hated not being capable, losing the function in his strongest arm, but getting angry about it didn't help his progress and he knew it. Sometimes he just forgot about it, and then he'd surprise himself all over again by not having the control he wanted.

He looked down at Jessica, sitting still, eyes fixed in the distance.

"You okay?"

It was as if she had to snap out of a trance before she even noticed he was speaking.

"Yeah."

Ryan watched as she jumped to her feet and brushed the grass off her jeans. "Yeah, I'm fine."

Maybe he'd been away way too long, or maybe he'd just forgotten how sensitive women were. Because they'd only been at the park less than an hour and already he'd done something to upset her.

And he had no idea what.

"You still want to grab some lunch?" he asked.

She smiled at him, this time more openly. Or maybe more guardedly. He couldn't tell which.

"Sure. Let's go."

Jessica couldn't fathom why her stomach was twisting like a snake had taken ownership of it. Why did it even bother her? So he was going back to war? He was a soldier and that's what soldiers did. It was just that she hadn't *expected* him to be going back. When he'd written to her and told her he was coming home she'd thought it was for good.

It wasn't as if he'd promised her something and was now going back on his word. She had no right to even feel this way.

They were friends.

So why was she acting like her lover had come home and lied to her about his intentions? Or maybe she'd just dealt with too much loss to even comprehend the thought of losing anyone else from her life again. She knew firsthand what the consequences were of him not coming home, what the risks were.

"You *sure* you're all right?" he persisted.

Jessica's head swivelled so quickly it almost swung off.

"Me?"

He laughed and she watched as he pushed his hands into his jeans pockets.

"Yes, you."

She felt the flush of her cheeks as he made fun of her. She'd expected him to be the one clamming up and here she was like a nervous bunch of keys being jangled. She hadn't even realized how long they'd been walking in silence.

"I'm sorry Ryan, it's just…"

He shrugged. "I took you by surprise."

This was a man who'd been away from civilization for years, and yet he seemed to have her all figured out. That made a change.

Jessica sighed.

"I understand if you don't want to, you know, hear about war or anything. It's not exactly the most pleasant experience to discuss," he said.

She frowned at the look on his face. It took her a second, because she hesitated, but Jessica reached for his hand to give it a quick squeeze. She was being stupid and he was the one who needed her to act like normal. To listen to him like she had in all their letters. He had no idea why she was affected by what he'd said, and that's how it had to be. She'd lost too much, exposed those she loved to that loss as well, and it had struck a chord with her. But that was one musical instrument she had no intention of playing around him, and that meant she had to deal with it and move on. Fast.

"You can tell me all you like, honestly. I just didn't expect you to be going back there anytime soon," she explained. "It took me by surprise."

Ryan caught her hand before she could pull it away. His hand was strong, smooth. And the touch made a tingle start in her fingertips and ripple goose bumps up her forearm.

"You're the only person I've been able to talk to, apart from the guys, since I left."

She nodded. Words refused to form in her throat. It had been so long since a man had touched her. Since she'd even felt a spark of attraction that had made her heart beat like a hammer was thwacking it from side to side.

"If I can't talk to you, I've got no one," he added.

Jessica couldn't take her eyes off their hands. Ryan followed her gaze and seemed to realize what the problem was, opening his grip and slowly releasing her fingers.

"I'm sorry," he muttered.

"Don't be sorry."

She smiled up at him. Watched the way his eyes crinkled ever so gently at the sides as he smiled back at her.

"Oh, no!" she exclaimed.

Ryan jumped to attention, eyes scanning, like he was looking for an enemy, but Jessica was already moving back toward the park.

"What?"

"Where's Herc?" she gasped.

Her heart had gone from thumping out of desire to banging from terror. How could she have been that distracted? How could she not have noticed that he'd wandered off? Her baby, her best friend, her...

Hercules had been there for her through everything. When she was home recovering, cuddling up by her side as the chemo ravaged her body. Snuggling her when she couldn't force herself out of bed in the morning. Listening to her as she'd sobbed after surgery.

He'd probably just wandered off in search of more ducks, chasing mallards again, but still...

Jessica had huge hot tears that felt like balls of fire fighting to get free of her lashes, desperate to spill, but she gulped them back, moving as fast as she could back the way they'd come.

She jumped as a hand came down on her shoulder. A hand that seemed to distribute calm energy through her body, grounding her, telling her everything was going to be okay.

"I'll run ahead, you keep your eyes peeled." Ryan's deep voice was commanding as he took charge. "I'll get him, you just stay calm."

Jessica nodded. She wasn't capable of doing anything else. Herc always followed along beside her off the lead, but then she wasn't usually so distracted.

She watched Ryan thump gracefully down the sidewalk, his feet beating a steady rhythm as he jogged away from her.

"Herc!" Jessica called as loud as she could. "Come on, Herc!"

Ryan had never felt as if his heart was actually in his throat before. Maybe at the funeral, when he'd had to watch his son cry as his mother was lowered in a coffin into her grave. But that was a different kind of emotion. That was pure agony, mourning like he'd never known he could experience.

This? This was desperation, panic. Determination to find what he was looking for.

He'd settled into a quick steady jog and he was almost back to where they'd come from, searching with his eyes as he moved. The dog had been at their side when they'd left but the little rascal must have skipped off when something caught his nose.

Then Ryan spotted him. A brown bullet barking his head off as he chased ducks back and forth along the bank again. Completely oblivious to the fact he was alone and had found his way back solo.

Phew.

"Hercules!"

The dog ignored him. Ryan kept running, slowing only to scoop the bundle of fur into his arms.

Hercules jumped and wriggled, but Ryan held him firm.

"You gave us a fright, bud."

The dog just wriggled some more, tongue flapping as he tried to contort his little body around so he could lick him. Ryan held him in an iron-tight grip, just far enough away so he could avoid being slobbered all over.

"Come on, let's go find your mom."

He started jogging again, until he spotted Jessica ahead. He would have waved but he was determined not to let the dog go. He was writhing like a slippery fish again.

When she saw them, Jessica's entire face lit up, a smile stretching across her lips.

"Herc!"

Ryan slowed and grinned. "Told you I'd get him."

Now she was crying. Oh, no, he didn't do tears well. He went to hold the dog out but she threw herself into his arms instead, almost making him drop the little animal!

"Thank you, Ryan. Thank you, thank you, thank you."

He gave her a half hug back, the other arm still occupied by Hercules.

Ryan went to move at the same time as she kissed him on the cheek. His face turned too far and she got him on the side of his mouth.

He fought not to turn farther into her, his pulse racing at her mouth on his.

"Oh."

He grimaced. "Sorry."

Jessica was bright red again, like a piece of freshly snapped rhubarb.

"I—"

He stepped back, clipped the dog onto the leash hanging from her hand and put him down.

"How about we head back to your place? Get him out of trouble?" he suggested.

Jessica nodded, still flushed.

He didn't know what was happening here, but one thing he did know was that somehow they weren't behaving like long lost pen pals. When she'd held him before, it had felt too warm. Like someone had shone the sun itself between them. Like they were the only two people in the world.

And if it had been another time and another place, he'd have been tempted to never let her go.

But he was only here for a few months. Maybe less. He'd come looking for her because she'd been such a wonderful support to him. Helped him talk about his feelings, open up.

Without her, he doubted he'd have ever have had the strength to come home, to face his demons once and for all.

There was no chance he was going to stuff this up by letting his emotions get the better of him. Jessica was off limits romantically.

And that was nonnegotiable.

He had to maintain their friendship, repair his relationship with his son and summon the strength to open up to his own parents. Tell them how much he appreciated them and what they'd done for him.

He grimaced at the thought of what the coming months held.

He'd just have to take it all one step at a time.

CHAPTER THREE

Dear Ryan,
I know you feel like you can't come back home,
but that's just fear talking. I'm not going to tell
you that soldiers shouldn't be fearful, because a
soldier is nothing more than a brave human being
and you can't help how you feel. But you need to
repair your relationship with your son while you
can. And you need to face the fact that he will
want to talk with you about his mother.

I don't know what you're going through, but I
do understand pain and loss. I know what it feels
like to grieve, and to want to hide away, but in
the end you have to be honest with yourself. It's
the only way forward.

Remember I'm here for you. If you need some-
one to hold your hand, that person can be me. No
questions asked.
Jessica

JESSICA HAD BEHAVED like a brainless airhead. Since when could she forget her dog? And the way she'd shut out Ryan after he'd opened up to her was unacceptable. He must think she was some kind of a nutcase. Not the level-headed pen pal who was full of wisdom that he'd come to rely on.

Nothing about today had gone as planned.

Jessica smiled as he walked back into the room. She swallowed away her fear and pinched her hand.

"Ryan, I'm so sorry."

He looked confused. One eyebrow raised slightly higher than the other. "What about?"

She sighed. He was either really good at pretending, or men actually were incredibly good at just letting things go.

"About before. Can we just start over? Go back to when you arrived?"

Ryan chuckled. He actually chuckled, while she stood there all breathless and red-faced.

"Whatever you say."

Argh! Men could be so irritating. He was just like her brother. Or worse. Acting like something hadn't happened when it had. But if he wanted to forget about it then she wasn't going to argue with him. She'd behaved badly and now she had a chance to make things right.

"Okay, how about we actually have a cup of something hot and make some lunch then?"

He grinned and walked right up to her, stopping a few feet back. Ryan held out his hand.

"I'm Ryan, it's so good to finally meet you."

She glared at him and stuck her hands in her pockets.

"Not funny, Ryan." The expression on his face didn't change. It was so serious he almost made her laugh, but she felt like too much of an idiot to shrug it off. "I made a fool of myself back there and it wasn't me. I mean, I don't even know how to explain myself."

He smiled at her again, but this time she didn't feel mocked.

"I thought you wanted to start over?"

Jessica turned away from him.

"Look, I took you by surprise, that's all. Now let's have some food, okay? I'm starving. Unless you want to meet all over again, again?" he teased.

Jessica sighed and walked back into the kitchen. Her face still felt flushed, but she was starting to relax. Lucky this was a friendship where they already kind of knew one another. If it had been a first date she'd have been toast.

"Can I do anything?" he offered.

She shook her head.

"I'll make some sandwiches and meet you outside."

When he didn't move she made herself look up at him.

"Hercules would love to play ball if you're up for a game in the yard," she suggested.

He winked at her and sauntered out the door.

Jessica had to force her mouth to stay shut. It was in grave risk of dropping down and hitting her on the chest.

Something about that man had her all twisted in knots, and that wink hadn't helped. She was all hot, like she needed a fan, but she gulped down a glass of water instead.

And it didn't help her any.

Ten minutes later, and still hot under the collar, Jessica found Ryan sitting back on one of her chairs, eyes closed, basking in the sun. A very put-out-looking Hercules lay nearby, ball neglected between his front paws.

She leant over to put the tray of food and drinks on

the table when Ryan's eyes popped open. He looked lazy, comfortable.

Gorgeous.

She pushed the thought away as he ran a hand through his hair and then down his face, as if to wake himself up.

"You've got no idea how good this is, just sitting here."

"Sandwich?"

He took it happily and started eating. Jessica made herself do the same, even though swallowing was like forcing large chunks through a sieve.

They sat in silence for a bit. Eating. Watching the dog chase his tail then start stalking a bird.

"Don't get me wrong, Jess, but I could have sworn you had something other than my going back to war on your mind before."

This time she actually choked. Had to reach for her coffee and take a big gulp. What had happened to the stereotype of brooding soldier who hardly said a word and wasn't up with the whole feelings thing? She had expected him to be quiet and reserved, but the reality of him was anything but. He'd either come out of his shell big-time, or he was making a huge effort here.

And hadn't they put this behind them and started over?

"Sorry, went down the wrong way," she stuttered.

Ryan didn't look convinced, just reached for another sandwich.

"Whatever you say."

She sighed.

"It's true I've had a lot going on this past year, but I just wasn't expecting to have to worry about you going back on top of it all. That's all."

It wasn't technically a lie. She *would* worry about him when he was gone. But when he'd told her, her mind had wandered. To a place she didn't want to go and shouldn't have let herself be drawn back to.

"Jessica?"

She put on the brave face she had perfected over the months of treatment she'd received and turned back to him.

"I'm fine, honestly. Tell me about you. What do you want to do while you're home? Do you need somewhere to stay?"

She held her breath, hoping he'd say no. There was no way she could deal with him staying here. Not now. It was messing her head up just trying to be normal around him for an afternoon.

"Tempting offer, but no, thanks."

She tucked her feet up beneath her on the seat and turned to face him. It was comforting in a way to watch his face, but off-putting at the same time. Hard to fathom this man sitting here was the author of all those letters, the ones that had kept her going, even through the hard times. Given her something to look forward to and something to focus on.

His eyes softened as he smiled, laughter lines etched ever so slightly into his tanned skin.

"I've been hoping you might have some good advice to throw my way." He paused, taking a sip of his coffee. "On how to deal with a twelve-year-old boy who can't seem to bear the sight of me."

Her heart throbbed for a moment, feeling his pain. But she recovered without him noticing.

"When you say he can't bear the sight of you…"

Ryan grimaced. "I mean that he gets up and leaves the

room the moment he sees me, or suffers my presence at mealtime by sitting silently and not raising his eyes."

Oh. "And your parents?"

That brought the smile back to his face. "Thrilled to have their only son home and desperate for me to reconnect with my own boy."

She thought about it for a moment. The nice thing about already having a relationship with someone, even if it was on paper, was that silent stretches weren't uncomfortable. Or at least they weren't with Ryan.

She unfolded her legs and leaned toward him.

"I know it's going to sound like a cliché, saying that you just need to give him time, especially after all the time you've been away, but I think he'll come around. He's probably angry at you for leaving and staying away so long, and he wants answers. You need to let him know that when he does want to ask you questions you can be there for him, straight up, honest."

Ryan closed his eyes and sat back. She could see this was painful for him, but he was better to get it all off his chest with her.

Besides, talking about him was taking her mind off the fact that she was attracted to him. That his being there, beside her, was making her have feelings she'd long ago abandoned when it came to men. And it also made her push her memories back where they belonged. Locked in a box, out of mind's reach.

He smiled sadly. "You're right, but sometimes I wonder if he'd have been better off if I'd just stayed away."

Jessica shook her head. It wasn't true and he knew it.

"Why don't you practice on me," she suggested, voice soft. "You can pretend I'm George."

He nodded. She only just registered the incline of his head as he moved it.

Jessica took a deep breath. "Okay, I'll start." She paused. "Why did you really go back to war so soon? Why didn't you come home? Stay with me?"

He kept his eyes shut. "I can't answer that."

She sighed and sat back. On second thought she reached for his hand, wanting to give him strength even if it hurt her. "If you can't be honest with me, how are you going to be honest with a boy who wants the truth?"

She watched as Ryan's thumb traced her palm, holding her hand back. It felt so good it hurt, but she didn't dare pull her hand away. Couldn't. The tingle in her fingertips and the pulse at her neck were enough to make her stay put.

When he was ready to talk he dropped his hold and pulled his chair around to face her head-on. She forced herself to breathe, had to concentrate on every inhale and exhale of her lungs.

"Okay, let's do this."

She nodded, still off balance from touching him, from his skin connecting with hers. From wanting him to do it again and hating herself for even thinking about him like that.

Ryan squeezed his eyes shut one more time then focused, looking firmly into hers.

"I left because going away was easier than staying. I was a coward and I should have been here for you."

Jessica gulped silently as tears pooled in her eyes. This was what he'd been needing to say for so long. There was no disguising the pain in his voice.

"Go on," she urged huskily.

"I told myself that you would be better off without

me, and I felt guilty over your mom's death. Like if only I'd loved her more, been here for her more, she could have pulled through. Everyone thought we had this perfect life, and in many ways we did, but then when she got sick everything just went into free fall, and after a while it was easier to just stay away than deal with her death." He paused. "And with you."

Jessica stood and walked away a few steps. She couldn't help it. Tears hit her cheeks and trickled their way down her jaw. She'd known hurt before, known what it was like to be left, but she also knew what it was like to be the one who did the hurting.

"Jess?"

"I'm sorry, it's just…"

"Did I say something wrong?" He sounded concerned.

She reached her fingertips to her face and brushed the tears away. Before she could turn large hands fell on her arms, holding her from behind.

"I shouldn't have said all that, but once I started it…"

Jessica closed her eyes then turned back to face him. She'd tried not to let her own feelings intrude, but it was hard. Impossible even.

"I lost someone once, too, Ryan, that's all. Hearing you say all that kind of brought that back. I don't know why but it did."

His eyes questioned her but he didn't say anything. Instead it was as if a metal guard had been raised, shielding his gaze and putting a wall between them. A divide that hadn't been there before.

Jessica didn't want to think about her past. Probably as much as Ryan wanted to disclose his, if the look on his face right now was any indication. It did give them something in common. Not exactly the common element most people would wish for, but on some level she did understand him. And if she wanted to tell him, he'd probably feel the same about her. But she didn't want to, and the last thing she intended was burdening him with her problems, or letting her mind dwell on what could happen to her.

"You know what? I think maybe it's time for me to go," he said, suddenly looking like a startled animal within sight of a predator. As if he wanted to flee the scene.

"Okay." Now she was the one confused. "Do you want to maybe grab dinner tonight? Do that 'start over' thing again?"

He was smiling but it looked forced. Not like before.

"Can we take a rain check on that? Maybe tomorrow night?"

Ouch. She hadn't seen that one coming. She'd over-reacted, not been able to keep her emotions in check, but she hadn't realized he'd react like that.

"How about you call me when you're free?" she suggested.

He nodded and turned back toward the house. "See you, bud."

At least he'd said goodbye to the dog.

"I'm sorry, Jess. It's just that I need to pick George up from school."

She shrugged. Even she knew that school didn't get out for a while yet. "I get it. We can catch up later."

She followed him back into the house, wondering what she would give to truly start over with him and be the strong girl from the letters. To go back to him standing on her doorstep and make the day turn out completely different.

His tall frame disappeared through the door and he didn't look back, his broad shoulders and dark hair fading from sight.

Jessica stood with her hands on her hips and surveyed the huge stretch of canvas on the floor in front of her. Not her best work, but the colors were brilliant. The organic paint took some getting used to, although if it meant no toxic fumes she had no intention of complaining.

She'd tried to focus on her new piece, but her mind kept wandering. Going to a place she didn't want to go back to but couldn't claw out from.

She found it was easier sometimes to pretend it hadn't happened. When you were surrounded by people who loved you or who had been the cause of grief, it sucked something from you. Pulled you into a world you didn't want to confront.

Like her cancer. She'd dealt with. Fought it. Survived it.

Yet her family treated her like she needed permanent wrapping in cotton wool just to survive each day now. Looked at her in a way that made her uncomfortable. And she hated it.

Was that how Ryan felt? The same way she did when she looked in the mirror and saw the reality of her body? Is that how he felt about being home? About the reality of what he'd gone through and then battled every day? How it was to come home and face something you'd run from for years?

Sometimes she felt like that, too. Sometimes she wished she could run away from what had happened and leave it all behind. But just like Ryan had had to return, so had she. To the reality of life as a cancer survivor.

She let her hand brush over the almost-hard contour of her breast, skimming the side of it, not caring that her fingers were covered in paint. Jessica sighed. She'd always mocked women with implants. Found it hard to fathom why breast augmentation was such an attraction.

She smiled with the irony. When she'd faced the reality of a double mastectomy, the first question she'd asked was what kind of reconstruction they could do. How they could give her her femininity back. Her breasts.

So now she had teardrop-shaped silicone implants that were better than nothing, but that still made her shake her head sometimes. That despite being diagnosed with cancer, facing chemo, knowing there was a chance she could die, all she'd wanted was to feel like a woman again. To know that even though they didn't feel soft when they'd once been natural, she still had her femininity, even if it had meant facing cosmetic reconstructive surgery to obtain them.

Maybe it was the same for Ryan. Without being a soldier, he would feel like less of a man, less of a human being. Maybe that was why he felt he had to go back, had to return to his unit. Had to offer himself up for redeployment.

If she could talk to him, explain to him how she felt, maybe it would help him. Help them both. But she couldn't do it.

She didn't want him to know. Couldn't tell him. Because then he'd start looking at her the same way everyone else did, and with Ryan, she just wanted to be Jessica. Not the girl with cancer. The girl in remission. Or the girl who'd already lost her sister to the disease.

Maybe he wouldn't look at her differently, or treat her like a different person, but she wasn't prepared to risk it. Not when she only had a limited time to enjoy having a friend like Ryan.

Or maybe she was too scared to tell him.

Either way, it was her secret and she had no intention of divulging it.

But after the way he'd left today, like he was fleeing a burning wreckage, she didn't know when they'd be seeing each other again. If ever.

"Jess?"

She looked up as Bella crossed her arms and leaned against the door of her studio. Jess sighed. Today had definitely not gone as planned.

"You have some serious explaining to do," her friend said.

CHAPTER FOUR

Jessica,
I don't know how you know so much about loss
or dealing with pain, but you've helped me more
than I could ever tell you. Having a friend to write
to, someone to just hang out with in the normal
world, makes all the difference to me. I love what
I do, wouldn't give it up for the world, but some-
times it helps to have someone non-army to talk
to.

You do realize I'm gonna owe you big-time
when I come home. Dinner, drinks, whatever
you want, but you writing to me has given me a
boost, and that only makes me a better soldier.
I was starting to think I was too old for war, but
it's like I've been recharged.

So think about it. When I finally leave this
place and come home, my shout. Whatever you
want. And I promise not to talk about me or ask
you for any more advice. Okay?
Ryan

RYAN SAT IN the car and watched the throng of kids
as they spilled out from the building. He couldn't see
George, but then that was hardly a surprise. The boy

would probably hide in class to avoid having to get in the car with his dad.

But Ryan was patient. He'd wait here as long as he had to. Besides, it wasn't as if he didn't have enough on his mind to keep him occupied.

Jessica.

Today had started out so well and ended so...badly. He closed his eyes and leaned back into the seat. He thumped his hand on the wheel. Ow! Sometimes he forgot he was meant to be recuperating, that he couldn't use his arm like that. It hurt badly sometimes, ached, bothered him when he was uptight or unsure.

He hated not being strong and capable. It wasn't that he was weak, but he'd always been the tough guy, the one who could be counted on physically and mentally in the worst of situations.

And it wasn't like it was only his arm troubling him. His head was messed up, too, especially after his behavior earlier.

Somehow he'd managed to screw today up. Jessica was supposed to be the easy part, the simple meeting of a friend. How wrong he'd been.

Why was being back so hard? He was so good at being a soldier, it came so naturally to him. Ryan swallowed and looked out the window.

Being a dad had come naturally to him once, too.

So had being a husband.

But that felt like another lifetime ago. Like he could just hold on to it as a long-distant memory, but it was starting to fade. Fast.

Ryan jumped at a knock on the car window.

He cursed, then pushed the button to wind down the window and acknowledge George's teacher. "You frightened the life out of me!"

"Sorry." The young man smiled, holding out his hand.

Ryan opened the door and got out, shaking the teacher's hand and leaning against the side of his car.

"It's Shaun, right?"

The teacher nodded. Ryan had only met him once before, on his first day back, but he'd liked him straight away.

"I saw you sitting here and thought I'd see how you were getting on with George," Shaun said.

Ryan shrugged. What did he say to that?

"Not great." There seemed no point in not telling the truth.

"Anything I can do to help?"

"You know, once upon a time I knew exactly what to say to make him laugh, just to be there for him. You know?" he said.

Shaun gave him a kind smile.

"It's not so easy anymore. Figuring out what the right thing to do with him is hard work," Ryan admitted.

"I'm sure you're doing everything you can. Just stick with it and do what feels right."

Ryan nodded, shoulders heaving as he exhaled. He wasn't usually one to open up, to talk to someone about how he felt, but George seemed to genuinely like his teacher. And he appreciated the offer of help.

"I guess I've found it hard to know what to say to him since his mom died. Until now, I've taken the easy way out and let my parents do the hard work."

It had indeed been the coward's way out and he was man enough to admit it. Especially now he could see firsthand the effect it had had on his boy.

"What matters is that you're here now and you want to do something about it." The teacher held out his hand again and patted Ryan on the shoulder with the other.

"You'll get there, and if you need someone to talk to—
either of you—I'm here. Okay?"

"Thanks."

Shaun gestured toward the door. "I saw him by his
locker before, I'm sure he'll be out soon."

Ryan watched the teacher walk off and got back in
the car.

When he'd been redeployed the last time, he was still
grieving for his wife. He'd held his son at the airport,
hugged him tight and then walked away. Seeing his own
mother hold his boy had left an image in his mind that
had never faded. An image that told him George would
be happier without his dad. That a messed-up, grieving, unsure father was nothing compared to the steady,
loving influence of grandparents.

And then every month he'd stayed away it had simply
been easier to keep telling himself it was true. That it
was better for George, and it was sure easier for him.
Because he didn't have to see the similarities to his wife
in his son's face on a daily basis. Didn't have to remember what it had been like when they'd been a family, the
three of them. Happy and content.

But now... Now George was, well, not a little boy
anymore. He'd gone from a sweet nine-year-old to an
almost twelve-year-old with a voice on the verge of
cracking and an attitude to boot. It was obvious he loved
his grandparents, but his feelings toward his father were
a whole other matter entirely.

If he even felt anything for his father anymore.

But what had Ryan expected? To come home and pick
up where they'd left off? He'd been a fool to stay away
so long, but he wasn't going to run away again. He was
going to stand up, take it on the chin and accept the fact
that he'd failed his son.

The car door opened. Ryan sat up straighter and looked into the eyes of his son.

George scowled at him and slammed the door, school bag on his knee.

"Hey."

George ignored him.

"Good day at school?"

Ryan received a shrug in return before George slumped down low and stared out the window.

He turned the ignition and pulled out into the traffic.

Part of Ryan wanted to explode. To pull over and grab his son and shake him until he listened. To tell him what he'd been through, how much he hurt, what he'd seen during wartime that had made his stomach turn.

"George…"

But he couldn't tell him off. Because his son had done nothing wrong. He was just behaving how any hurt child of his age would. By dishing out the silent treatment. So Ryan clenched all his fingers around the wheel and kept his eyes on the road and his mouth shut.

George didn't seem to have noticed he'd even been spoken to. But a letter every other week and a dad absent for almost two years since his last trip home meant that Ryan deserved the silent treatment. The short time he'd spent with him between deployments the last time had been strained and emotional, but George had been a lot younger then. More accepting and so excited to have his dad back.

So right now he needed to wait it out, or figure out a way to make amends. It wasn't as if he could jump up and down and insist the boy behave. George was on his way to becoming a young man, and if he didn't fix things between them soon, he might lose his chance forever.

But this wasn't the army. And George wasn't his subordinate.

He was a dad and he had a lot to prove before he deserved the title. Being a father wasn't something you could write on a name tag and lay claim to. He'd been anything *but* a dad these past few years, and it was embarrassing. Ryan had grown up in a loving family, his parents had been married thirty-seven years and his own father had been a shining role model.

Ryan felt his knuckles harden, like he was trying to squeeze the lifeblood from the steering wheel.

He'd let his own dad down, too, as much as he'd let himself down. After having the best example set for him, Ryan had ignored his instincts, that gut feeling that he was behaving badly. Had left it way too long to make amends.

Which is why part of him wanted to run back to the army and write this entire episode off as too hard. Hide again because it was easier.

But he'd promised himself he wouldn't do that. Because this time he had to face up to his past, to what had happened, and try to move forward. Instead of sticking his head in the sand like a stubborn ostrich.

Ryan flexed his jaw. The kid still hadn't made a noise.

"What do you think about grabbing something to eat?"

George didn't look at him, eyes still trained out the window, like he couldn't think of anything worse than being in an enclosed space with his father, let alone having to communicate with him.

"Or would you rather go home?" Ryan asked.

"Home."

Ryan nodded. At least he'd spoken. But he knew the

drill. They'd arrive home, George would kiss his grand-mother on the cheek and grab a handful of her baking, then head to his room. He'd either push his headphones on and blast music through his eardrums like he was determined to be deaf before his eighteenth birthday, or go square-eyed playing video games.

He had intended on asking George if he wanted to do something tonight, but that clearly wasn't going to happen.

Which meant maybe, just maybe, he should call Jessica.

Jessica.

Now that was one word that was always sure to put a smile on his face. He had grinned like an idiot when-ever a letter had arrived for him with her unmistakable handwriting on the back. And when he'd seen her today, he could barely wipe the smile from his lips.

He'd been rude earlier, hot then cold, and he had no idea why she'd rattled him so bad. Seeing her cry had done something to him, made him remember what it was like to see his wife cry. Years of her being the strong pillar of their marriage had fallen like dust to the ground that day they'd found out she'd had cancer. And seeing Jessica cry today had messed with his head in the same way.

But she had seemed on edge, too, before she'd broken down. Not herself, if that was even possible for him to know when he'd never met her before. But all those letters, all those words they'd shared, they counted for something. And deep down something was telling him that she would be just as annoyed with herself as he was with himself right now.

Which meant there was a glimmer of hope that she'd give him another chance and agree to the dinner she'd suggested before he'd blown cold and fled like a pride of lions was in pursuit of his soul.

Ryan sighed and pulled into the driveway of his parents' house.

He'd already made a mess of his relationship with his son, but he didn't have to ruin the one good thing in his life right now. Jessica was a great friend, *had* been a great friend, and he wasn't going to act like an idiot and face the prospect of going back to war somewhere without knowing her letters would follow him there.

Wherever in the world he'd been, wherever they'd sent him, her letters had always found him. And she had no idea how that had kept him going. Kept him alive when everything else had gone so wrong.

He glanced at George again and noticed his eyes had closed. Great, now he preferred being unconscious to being in the car with his dad.

There was no chance of them spending time together tonight, so he wasn't going to beat himself up about going out on a date.

Ryan clasped the wheel harder and stared straight ahead.

Not a date. Not in any way a date.

He was going to ask a friend for dinner. They'd already discussed it earlier.

Just because she looked incredible did not mean it was a date by any stretch of the word.

He ground his teeth together.

George leaped from the car with the most enthusiasm Ryan had seen from him all day as soon as they were stationary.

Dinner with Jessica was definitely his best option.

* * *

Jessica couldn't stop stirring her coffee. It was the only way she could continuously avoid her friend's stare.

"You can't avoid me forever."

That was the problem. Bella had been her best friend far too long to be put off so easily. But what could she tell her? The truth was she had no idea herself what had happened.

"So what did he look like?"

Jessica took a sip and ignored the way the liquid burned her mouth.

"He was, um, normal. You know? Just a regular guy."

She looked down again. If normal guys had frames that could fill doorways without an inch of fat covering their bones. Sharp blue eyes that made her want to blush every time they were turned her way, or tanned skin that seemed like the sun itself had fallen to earth to kiss it.

"Normal?" Bella didn't sound convinced.

Jess nodded.

And received a punch to the arm in response.

"You're lying." Then Bella poked her, hard. "You know you can't lie to me!"

Jess sighed. "Okay, so he was good-looking, but it doesn't matter anyway."

Bella started to laugh. "Mmm, so the fact that your soldier was hot didn't interest you at all?"

Jessica felt her cheeks burn. They heated up so fast it was as if a fire had been lit in her mouth.

"Bella, we both know I'm not interested. He's a friend, nothing more." She did her best to sound firm. Assertive.

It didn't come naturally to her. Not given the current subject matter.

"Did you like him, though? I mean, if you weren't all hung up on not getting involved with someone…"

Jessica didn't like where this conversation was going. Not at all.

"Theoretically, yes." She held up her hand as Bella got that look on her face. That look that made her appear like an overexcited Labrador dog. "But that's irrelevant because I'm *not* interested in men. Period."

Bella didn't seem put off. "Did you find out if he was being redeployed anywhere?"

Jessica felt her skin prickle, like a hedgehog had rolled over her arms, making goose pimples appear. She didn't want to think about Ryan being sent back to his unit. Wherever in the world that might be, she knew in her gut it would be dangerous.

She nodded. "Yeah, he's going back."

"So let me get this right." Bella grinned and shuffled her chair closer. "You're telling me that the guy was gorgeous, you were attracted to him and he's only here for a short time?"

Jess *definitely* didn't like where this was going. She didn't even bother replying. It wasn't as if Bella was about to start listening to her now. She never had before.

"So can you explain to me why you don't want to jump his bones?"

She sighed. Did that type of question even warrant a response? So she'd thought about him *like that*. He was attractive, yes. He was charming. He was, well, *nice*. Better than nice. Wonderful.

But it still didn't mean she was going to let something happen romantically. She'd promised herself no men, no complications, no romance.

So why would she consider breaking her rules now for him?

"Jess?"

She shook her head. "I'm just not interested in Ryan or anyone else for that matter. Not now."

"You're missing the point, Jess." Bella reached over the kitchen counter and took hold of her friend's hand. "We're talking about a guy who's only going to be here for a short time, *before he's sent miles away.* It's not like it would be something long-term." She paused. "You could let your hair down, forget all about what's happened and just live in the now for a while."

Jessica didn't want to hear this. She wished she could close her ears and sing loudly like a naughty child who refused to listen until her friend shut up. Only they weren't children and Bella kind of had a point. But it didn't matter what she said or how tempting it might sound. She was a cancer survivor. She had to focus on her health. On her future.

On protecting her heart.

And she didn't want to ruin her friendship with Ryan. What they had might be paper-based, but it meant a lot to her.

"Well?"

"No."

Bella rolled her eyes. "Give me one good reason?"

The phone rang. Jessica had never been so pleased for an interruption. Its shrill bleeping made her jump to her feet.

"Hello," she answered.

"Hey, Jess, it's Ryan."

The deep baritone that hit her eardrums sent a lick of excitement down her spine. She could curse Bella for putting ideas in her head!

"Hi, Ryan."

There was a pause. A silence that made her heart pound hard.

"I was, ah, wondering if you wanted to have dinner tonight after all?"

Jessica made the mistake of looking up at Bella. Her friend looked like she needed a paper bag, as if she were on the verge of hyperventilating.

"Is it him?" Bella was mouthing at her.

She nodded then turned her back. "Sure."

Now Bella was flapping her hands. She was in danger of becoming airborne.

"Quiet," Jess mouthed as she turned back, but her friend wasn't listening.

"Shall I pick you up around seven?"

"Sounds great. I'll see you then."

As she hung up Jessica looked at Bella.

"Well?"

Jess gulped. "We're going out for dinner."

"Yaaaaaay!"

She cringed at Bella's high pitch. She should never have told her.

"I can't believe you're finally back in the game." Her friend sighed with satisfaction. "Going out on a date."

Jess wished a hole would open up in the carpet and swallow her. Just suck her up and eat her whole. This was not a date. Absolutely *not* a date. No way.

"What are you going to wear?"

Jess groaned. Who was she kidding? This was absolutely a date. It didn't matter what she tried to pretend, or how she thought about it. She was a girl going out for dinner with a boy, her stomach was leaping around as if something with wings had taken ownership of it, and Ryan had sounded as unsure as she had felt herself on the phone.

Given that she'd promised herself there was to be no dating for five years, she'd broken her one rule pretty fast.

But maybe Bella was right. If something did happen between them, if she did want something to happen, would it be so bad? Ryan wasn't hanging around for long, there was no chance she could have her heart broken or get into something long-term, because he wouldn't even be here beyond a couple of months.

"Come on, let's get you ready."

She looked at Bella and tried not to get excited. Ryan would be here in a few hours. She'd be getting in his car, sitting across from him at a restaurant somewhere, looking into those sparkling blue eyes...

Jess groaned again, even more loudly.

So much for thinking of him as nothing more than a friend.

Jessica wished she could quell the inconsistent thudding of her heart, but she couldn't. It was no use.

She was nervous. Terrified. And for some reason there was nothing she could do to calm her nerves, her fear *or* her excitement.

If Bella hadn't kept insisting it was a date...

Argh. The word kept circling her brain like an eagle hunting prey. It wasn't a date. So why—the more she thought about the word—did it seem she was trying to convince herself of a cold-edged lie?

Jess parted the blinds to look out at the street. She watched as a couple of cars passed. The third one slowed then pulled up outside her house. Her hand dropped away, as if she'd been burned.

It was like this morning all over again.

Except this time she didn't want to run from the scene. This time she wanted to run into his arms.

She growled at herself. She needed to stop listening to Bella.

But despite all her reasoning to the contrary, her promises to herself, the truth was that she was tempted. He *was* going away again soon. And she *was* attracted to him. So if he was interested in her *like that* then didn't she owe it to herself to have a good time?

The logical part of her brain was telling her no. That his friendship meant too much to throw it all away. To even risk the possibility of something happening.

But the other part? That was telling her to have fun. To let her hair down for once. To enjoy the company of a man who didn't know any of her baggage, her past. Who didn't want to treat her as if broken glass was shattered over her skin, like he could hurt her.

That part knew that maybe, just maybe, this was an opportunity to be herself. A woman who wasn't afraid of moving forward and having fun. For the short term anyway.

Jess straightened her shoulders and ran her hands down her jeans. She wasn't going to wait for him to knock this time. Her poor heart couldn't handle it.

It had been a long time since Ryan had felt like he couldn't settle his nerves. His career depended on it. When he was deployed, he always kept calm, had a confidence and calmness that saw him through any scenario.

So when Jessica walked out onto the porch and gave him a half wave, before turning to lock the door, he was taken by surprise. It felt like someone had placed a steady hand around his throat and squeezed, just for a moment, to make him gasp for the next gulp of air. Made his mind scramble, as if he were incapable of utilizing the rational, functioning part of his brain.

Jessica had to fiddle with the lock and it gave him time to watch her. This girl who'd meant so much to him for so long.

He'd known he would feel close to her, but he hadn't expected this. He'd thought she would be a normal American girl, just another person in the world. The kind of girl you'd pass in the street and not necessarily notice.

How wrong he'd been.

Her hair was messy, as if she'd spent hours at the beach to put the wind through it and then played with each strand through her fingers. It was tousled and slightly curly, falling below her shoulders. Her skin was golden, as if the sun had just been allowed to skim it, and… He gulped.

Looking any further wasn't going to help him. The curve of her backside in her denim jeans, the silhouette of her upper half in her summery top.

He swallowed again, hard, when she turned to face him. Jessica was smiling, her full lips pulled back to show off white teeth, eyes slightly downcast as if she was a touch embarrassed.

Any thought of her being "just a friend" fled his mind.

It wasn't because he'd been away serving. It wasn't because he hadn't been around women in a long while.

It was simply Jessica.

She did something to him, scrambled his brain and made his body jump, like he'd never experienced before.

Ryan leaped from the car. He couldn't have moved faster if it had been on fire. It was like his brain and his body were finally capable of acting as one.

"Hey."

Jessica's cheeks were touched with the lightest of pink blushes.

"Hey," she said back.

He walked forward, wanted to kiss her on the cheek, but felt awkward. They stood, watched one another for a moment, before he stepped back.

Idiot.

"Let me get the door." Suddenly he was all nerves, more thumbs than fingers as he walked around to the passenger side.

She walked past him and ducked to get into the car. "Thanks."

He grinned at her, he could feel the goofy smile on his face and was incapable of doing anything to remove it.

Jessica looked up at him, her own face open, expectant.

"Let's go grab some dinner," he said.

She nodded at him, before he closed the door.

Ryan walked slowly back around to the driver's side and tried to pull himself together. He had possibly the most beautiful woman he'd ever met sitting in his car, waiting for him to be charming, expecting the person she'd met on paper, and he could hardly string a sentence together.

Jessica had looked good earlier today, but he hadn't had the chance to just watch her and drink her in.

He got in the car and pulled on his seat belt.

Ryan could feel her, smell her, sense her beside him. He made himself look over at her and smile. Ignored the insistent thump of his pulse, or his heart near beating from his chest and tried to act relaxed.

"We doing that 'start over' thing again?"

He smiled at Jessica's joking tone.

"We don't need to start over." He turned the ignition. "It was just, well, kind of weird meeting after knowing each other on paper for so long. Don't you think? We both sort of overreacted."

Jessica sighed. "Thank goodness we're on the same page."

He laughed at the same time she did. Their eyes met and they laughed some more. It was as if all the worry had vanished, the knot of uneasiness in his stomach had been untied. Just from hearing her laugh, knowing she felt the same way.

"Excuse the pun," Jessica managed to say, when they'd stopped laughing.

Ryan resisted the urge to reach for her hand, to make a connection with her. It was so unnatural for him to even think like that, but with Jessica it felt natural.

"We're going to have a good time tonight."

She leaned back in her seat, body angled to face him. "I think so, too."

Ryan chanced a quick glance at his passenger. She was looking out the window now.

He dragged his eyes back to the road.

Maybe coming home was the best thing he'd ever done.

Jessica smiled. She couldn't have wiped the grin from her face if she wanted to.

This morning, she'd been a bundle of nerves. She hadn't been much better this afternoon. But seeing Ryan again, being with him, something about it felt so right.

They shared an understanding, had a bond that was hard to describe.

And Bella had been right.

She *was* attracted to him.

It didn't mean she wanted something to happen between them. But maybe she did have to listen to her friend. She'd been celibate for well over a year now, had pledged not to put her heart in harm's reach or let someone else suffer because of what she might have to go through in the future.

But if Ryan was only here for a short time, who was she to say no to a romantic fling?

Jessica glanced over at Ryan, watched his strong hands grip the wheel, his jaw strong and angled and freshly shaved.

There was nothing not to like about him.

So if she couldn't get hurt or hurt him in return, what was the harm in admitting it?

CHAPTER FIVE

Dear Ryan,
I still can't believe we grew up so close together.
Not much has changed here since you've been
gone, well at least not that I can think of. I often
wonder about traveling, but I'm such a homebody.
I like being surrounded by family and doing the
same old thing, but sometimes, well, sometimes
I think it would be nice to run away for a bit,
even for a week or two. Step out of my life and be
someone else, just another traveler in a foreign
place.
Jessica

"I THOUGHT YOU said nothing much had changed around
here."

Ryan raised an eyebrow as he looked at her before
diverting his gaze. He was looking at a new electronics
store, which was certainly not the restaurant he'd been
expecting.

"Hmmm, maybe I hadn't realized quite how long
you'd been away." She bit her lip to stop from smiling.

"I can't believe the little Italian place has gone. It was
my favorite." He sighed and put the car in gear again.
"When I was away I'd dream of their bruschetta and

pasta, or watching their pizzas come out of the oven while we waited."

Now he had her mouth watering.

But, hang on…

"Do you mean Luciano's?"

Ryan's eyes flashed. "Sure do."

Jessica fought the urge to laugh again. The look on his face was priceless. "It might not be as good, but do you mind if I choose where we go?"

Ryan shrugged. "Sure."

"Turn left up here, then keep going straight."

He obeyed, pulling the car back out into the traffic.

"You go to this place often?"

Jessica shook her head. "No, but I've heard about it."

"Up here?"

"Yep, keep going and then pull into any spot past the next set of lights."

When the car was stationary Jessica grabbed her bag and opened the door. She had gotten the hint earlier that Ryan was a little old-fashioned about manners, but she couldn't wait to get out. To lead him to the restaurant. There was no time to wait for him to get her door.

"So where exactly are we heading?"

Ryan had one hand slipped into his jeans pocket. He looked strong, completely unflappable. He had dark eyebrows, and they were pulled together now, as if he was wondering what to say to her. His almost-black hair was tousled, just-got-out-of-bed messy. Not the cropped soldier look she had expected. There were two buttons of his shirt undone, the sleeves were rolled up to expose his forearms, and his tanned, soft skin was doing something to her insides. To her brain.

Jessica forced her eyes from him. Drinking in the sight of him was way too easy to do.

"This way."

He followed. They fell into step beside one another. It was weird, this feeling that she was out with a friend, yet the pair of them behaving somehow like it was more of a date than a casual outing.

"Ryan, can I ask you a question?"

He glanced at her as they walked. "Shoot."

"You've only just come back, but your hair is, well, normal. I thought you'd have a buzz cut."

Ryan laughed. "Not in special forces. Well, not all the time."

Now she was confused. "Huh?"

He had both hands pushed into his jeans pockets now, his long legs going slow so as not to outwalk her.

"We often have to look the part, you know, fit in wherever we're posted."

She liked how comfortable the air felt between them. Like they could talk about anything. That's how it had always felt when they wrote to one another, like they could open up about whatever was troubling them. No matter what.

"Let's just say you wouldn't have recognized me when I was away this time. I had a full beard and my hair was long and shaggy."

"What!"

"We often have to blend in. The last thing you want is your buzz cut marking you as U.S. Army. That way we're in less danger, because we're not likely to create attention. I have to go completely undercover as a sniper sometimes, and that usually means making sure no one notices me."

Jessica giggled. She couldn't help it.

"So you looked like a hobo?"

Ryan nudged her, bumped his arm into her shoulder.

Jessica kept her eyes downcast, was too afraid to look up. His touch, the strength of his upper arm as it skimmed hers, made her stomach flip.

"Slow down."

He did.

Jessica indulged in the pleasure of closing her hand over his forearm, let the warmth of his skin tingle through hers. It had been a long time since she'd touched a man, and even longer since the feel of another human being had made her feel like this.

"We're here."

The restaurant had a full glass frontage, a podium outside with the menu displayed and the unmistakable red-and-white checked tablecloths of an Italian restaurant.

"This isn't…"

Jessica squeezed his arm and dragged him inside.

"Luciano's."

Ryan stopped and stared into the restaurant. She loved the wide smile on his face, the way his eyes were dancing. Seeing happiness in another was something that never ceased to warm her heart.

"Wow."

"Not quite the little old restaurant you remembered, but let's hope the food hasn't changed."

She went to walk inside but Ryan's grip stopped her. Suddenly it was him holding her, his skin possessing hers rather than the other way around.

"Thank you."

Jessica refused to drop her eyes, to look at his hand. She made herself be brave, didn't let her nerves stop her.

Because she wanted this. She didn't want him to think she didn't.

"No problem."

Ryan stared at her, his eyes never leaving hers for what felt like forever.

"Table for two?"

Jessica turned, the spell broken. A waiter stood before them in the doorway, menus in hand.

"Ah, sure."

She felt Ryan follow her, his big body close behind hers.

She glanced at him as they sat at a small table in the corner, tucked near the window. He smiled.

And she knew then that everything had changed.

Because from the look on his face, the way his eyes looked like a storm was brewing but at the same time sunlight was shining through them, made her realize that maybe he was having the same internal battle she was.

That they were supposed to be friends and yet within a few hours the goalposts had moved.

But it wasn't just a new set of rules. It felt like a new game entirely.

One that she hadn't played before. Or at least not in a very long time.

Ryan sat back and studied Jessica.

He was confused. More than confused. He had no idea what he was doing or what he should do, and it wasn't a feeling he was used to.

This woman was doing something to him and he was helpless to stop it happening. In fact, he didn't want to stop it. With everything else that was going on, with his son and his arm, this was a pleasant distraction.

He watched as she glanced up, long lashes hiding her eyes when she quickly looked back down.

She was as nervous and uncertain as he was, there was no mistaking it, and it felt good. He liked that she was unsure, too. He was as confused as a guy could get over what was happening here, so he couldn't have handled her being Little Miss Confident. Her shyness made him want to step up and protect her, but not like it had been with his wife near the end.

He never wanted to feel helpless like that again. Like no matter what he did he couldn't protect the person he loved. That he was useless and not strong enough to make a difference, to save that someone.

With Jessica it was different. He wanted to protect her, the animal within him wanted to growl like a tiger and keep her to himself, but it wasn't because she needed protecting.

Jessica was strong. Healthy. Happy.

All he needed to do was enjoy her company, and humor the alpha inside of him that wanted to be released.

Ryan grinned when she glanced up at him again.

"Seen anything you like the look of?"

He didn't miss the instant flush as it hit her cheeks.

"Ah…"

He shook his head. That had come out all wrong. From the look on her face, she liked what she saw as much as he did when he watched her.

"I'm going to go with good old spaghetti bolognese," he said.

Ryan watched as she let out a breath and placed her hands over the menu.

"Meatballs for me, please."

He raised an eyebrow. "Good choice."

They watched one another. For a heartbeat that seemed like forever. Until she spoke, as if scared to just sit there and not say anything.

"How did you get on with George this afternoon?"

Ryan shook his head. "Not great. He's still not talking to me."

She smiled. "You'll get there with him. Have faith."

Faith. He'd kept the faith his entire time away, but at times, well, when he thought about his late wife or the way he'd run from his family, he wondered if he had any at all. What he'd seen away serving, what he'd had to witness, had made him question everything he'd ever known or believed in.

But sitting here with this sweet, charming woman now…it made him want to believe all over again. That he could be the man he'd been before experiencing loss. Before serving his country for so long.

That maybe, just maybe, before he went back the next time to rejoin his unit, he could be the man he'd like to be again in the future.

"Jess, about earlier today…"

"Water under the bridge." She put her hand up. "I asked for a chance to start over already, now you've had one. Consider us even."

He smiled at her; it was all he ever seemed to do when he was with her.

"Seeing you, well, emotional like that, it reminded me of a time I usually try to forget. I shouldn't have reacted like that," he apologized.

She reached out to touch his hand, the softest of touches, but enough to tell him that she was there for him. That she understood. "You mean your wife?"

Ryan swallowed what felt like a solid piece of gum in his throat. It shouldn't be so hard to go back there in his mind, not after all this time, but whenever he thought of the end, of what had happened, it was as if his mind put up an impenetrable shield.

"What I saw my wife go through took something from me." He paused. Jessica's hand was still hovering. "I couldn't ever go through seeing someone I care about experience that kind of pain again. Cancer is like a snake, it sneaks up on you, and once you're in its grip I don't know if you can ever be released."

He watched as Jessica's face froze. Only for a second, but he saw it. Saw something cross her eyes and her mouth, something that he couldn't put his finger on.

Her hand rose then fell back to his again, before she pulled it back entirely. Her face was back to normal but something had made her waver.

"I didn't know your wife died of cancer," she said.

Ryan nodded. Had he never told her in all those letters how she'd died?

"Seeing someone you love battle with it, well, I can't think of anything worse a person could go through."

The smile she gave him was tight, strained, but he'd probably just made her uncomfortable. Bringing up terminal cancer as a subject made people react differently. He should have realized that.

"Ryan, didn't you mention something about bruschetta before?"

His mouth watered. "Sure did."

"Why don't we share it? See if it's as good as it used to be."

Ryan raised his glass, pleased to see the sparkle back in her eyes, that sweet, natural smile back on her lips.

"To old times," he said.

"To friendship."

They clinked their glasses together, before he took a long sip of red wine from his.

It was good. Better than good.

This whole night felt great.

"I'll only say yes to bruschetta if we can finish the night with gelato," he teased.

Jessica sat back, wineglass tucked in her hand. "You're lucky I like my food."

They both laughed.

He'd done the right thing, inviting her out tonight. If they stayed just friends, then he'd be happy. But if something more happened…Ryan took another sip of wine before leaning in closer to Jessica across the table.

If something else happened then he wasn't going to say no.

He'd have to be a stronger man to resist. And after years of not being interested like this in a woman, it felt seriously good.

Jessica smiled at Ryan as he attempted to cut a huge piece of bruschetta, piled high with tomato, onion and basil. Her insides felt kind of fluttery, her brain kept firing her warning signals that she was electing to ignore, but she was still enjoying herself.

Hearing Ryan open up about his wife, hearing the dreaded *C* word…it had rattled her. She knew he'd noticed the look on her face, seen the blood drain from her skin temporarily, but she'd managed to recover fast enough that he hadn't called her out on it.

But still. Cancer? Part of her was pleased she'd never told him. After the way he'd talked about what he'd gone through, talked about what he *never wanted to go through again,* it had been clear he might not be sitting with her right now if she'd been honest from the beginning. He might not have even wanted to write to her if she'd told him.

But her chance to confess, to share what she'd been through, had passed. There had been a moment, a tiny window of opportunity, where she could have stopped him and told him what had happened to her. But she hadn't.

And she had no intention of telling him now. Maybe not ever.

"Jessica?"

She looked up. Ryan was watching her.

"This is delicious."

Jess reached for the large piece of bruschetta he had sliced off for her. The smell of the balsamic alone had her mouth watering. She could feel him watching her as she took a bite, trying to be dainty but struggling given the portion size.

"Mmmmm." She finished her mouthful. "You're right, it is delicious."

When he smiled at her, before finishing what was left on his plate like it was no more than a snack, she knew deep down that she couldn't tell him. If he was only here for a short time, who was she to be the one responsible for turning that happy smile into a frown? Why should her problems—health problems she'd dealt with on her own—be a reason not to have fun with him?

It wasn't like she was embarking on a long-term future with the man. They were friends, and friends kept their secrets sometimes. It just so happened this was one she didn't want to share with anyone who didn't already know about it.

"More wine?"

Jessica internally shrugged off her fears and eliminated all thoughts of Ryan's earlier words.

This was about having fun. Enjoying herself with a handsome soldier who would be back with his unit before the year was out.

"Please," she said recklessly, holding up her glass.

Ryan tipped the bottle of red and filled her glass to the halfway mark.

She took a long, slow sip, and leaned across the table toward him. "Tell me all about the guys you serve with. I want to know what it'll be like for you going back to them."

Jessica twirled her fingers around the long stem of her glass as Ryan sat back, his body relaxed against the chair.

"I don't know how exciting a story it is," he protested.

She shook her head, laughing as he grimaced. "You're not getting off that easily, and we've got all night."

"So gelato, huh?"

Ryan laughed. He seemed to do a lot of that around her.

"Believe me, when you're hot and sticky in the desert, thinking about gelato is like torture."

"And now you finally get to indulge."

He passed her the waffle cone before reaching back for his own. They were only a few blocks from where the car was parked, close enough to walk.

"Good?"

"Mmmmm."

Jessica was too busy swirling her tongue around the Italian ice cream to answer. She just kept making the noise in her throat to indicate how tasty it was.

Ryan gulped and tried to focus on his own dessert. But dragging his eyes from her mouth, from her tongue and the way her eyes were dancing as she watched what she was eating...

She looked up.

Whoops. Caught out like a dog trying to sneak a leg of lamb from the kitchen bench.

He watched in fascination as this time her throat worked slowly, swallowing, running her tongue over her lips then letting her hand drop lower as if she'd forgotten the gelato completely.

Ryan wanted to look away. He tried, he really did. But he found his body moving instead, toward her. The look in her eyes tormented and taunted him, pulled him into her web. He had to fight not to drop his cone to the ground.

Ryan could hear his own breathing, and he could hear hers, too. It was as if there was nothing else in the world around them, like they were the only two people on the street, in this moment.

He raised his arm, high enough to reach out and touch her face, and wiped the tiniest bit of ice cream from Jessica's mouth. Maybe he had imagined it, maybe he'd gently wiped away nothing. Maybe he just wanted an excuse to get closer to her, to be pulled toward her like a magnet to metal.

His arm ached, he felt a dull throb as he held it up, but he didn't care. He'd felt worse, and she was worth it. Touching her was worth any lick of pain, no matter how bad.

"Thanks," she whispered, eyes flickering low then higher again.

Ryan stood there. He gave her the chance to walk away, to move back so their bodies weren't so close. When she didn't he closed in, stepped forward and leaned toward her. She was tall but not as tall as him, the top of her head just higher than his chin.

"Jess," he murmured.

She nodded.

He pushed her arm down slightly, so she had to move her cone away from her body. It allowed him to get closer. Their chests were close, hovering, but not pressed together.

Ryan dipped his head, waited in case she wanted to move away. But she didn't.

Jessica raised her chin, inclined it up toward him.

He took a deep breath, looked at her mouth, couldn't pull his eyes away, then dropped his mouth to hers. Gently, ever so gently, he brushed his lips across Jessica's.

She tasted sweet, intoxicating. Gelato mixed with the warmth of a woman who wasn't sure, who wasn't used to being kissed in the street on a first date.

Ryan couldn't pull away, couldn't force his feet back. Instead he pressed their bodies that little bit closer, and touched his lips to hers again, more firmly this time.

Jessica couldn't breathe. She was finding it hard enough staying upright, let alone making her lungs work.

His lips fell on hers again, brushing, teasing, tasting. She couldn't help the tiny moan that escaped her mouth. Ryan's lips were soft yet strong, gentle yet firm, and it was turning her body into jelly.

He slowly pulled his lips away, raised his head high enough to look into her eyes.

"Hey," he whispered.

"Hey," she managed to reply.

They stood like that, bodies pressed together, neither ready to back away.

Ryan cleared his throat.

"I think your gelato's dripping down my arm."

"Oh!" Jessica jumped back and worked to clean up her cone, to stop the drips.

"Napkin?"

She nodded.

He walked back over to the ice cream vendor and retrieved a handful of paper napkins.

They wiped at their cones and started to eat them again, standing like a pair of teenagers who had no idea what to say to one another after their first kiss.

Jessica's body was singing, talking to her like a record on repeat. Telling her how good that had felt.

She'd just been kissed like she'd never been kissed before in her life. Her body was tingling, her skin on fire, alive. And her lips were tender from the thorough way his lips had danced over hers.

When Ryan grinned at her she couldn't help but do the same back.

"Shall we head back to the car?" he asked her.

Jessica nodded. And when he reached for her hand and took it against his big palm, she didn't resist. His skin was smooth but worn, a testament to the work he did.

Now there was no mistaking it.

This was definitely, without a doubt, one hundred percent a date.

Jessica wondered if it was possible for a heart to beat so hard that it could pump right through a chest cavity.

It didn't matter what she did, hers was heaving away so madly she could barely concentrate. She only hoped Ryan couldn't hear it.

He walked around and opened the door. This time

when he'd pulled up, she'd sat there in her seat, hadn't moved. And now he was towering above her.

Jessica gulped and forced herself to step out. She was torn. Part of her wanted another breathtaking, spine-numbing kiss. For Ryan to hold her in his arms and cocoon her, wrap her tight against him and kiss the breath from her over and over again.

But the other part told her to scurry inside her house as fast as she could. To never look back and to forget what had happened. No letting herself hope. Or think about what he'd said in the restaurant. Because no matter how much she liked him or wanted to take things further, his words had echoed in her mind over and over, reminding her of what he'd been through, telling her to be careful.

Reminding her of what he never wanted to go through again.

And it made her feel like she was deceiving him.

"It was great seeing you tonight, Jess."

Ryan held out his hand and she took it. Tried to ignore the tingle she felt when their skin connected.

He didn't let go.

"I had a really good time." Her voice was failing her, going all soft and breathy, but she couldn't help it.

He twisted her hand gently so their palms fell together and pushed the door shut with his other.

Ryan walked her up the path to her front door, slowly. "Good enough that you don't want it to end?"

"Yeah," she admitted. Only she couldn't ask him in. She wasn't ready for what it might mean or what he might think it meant.

"Can I call you tomorrow?"

Jessica was relieved he wasn't going to ask if he could

come in. She would have been powerless to say no if he'd given her the option.

"Until tomorrow," she agreed.

"Well, I guess it's good night then," he murmured.

Jessica tried not to wriggle. He still had hold of her hand, was turning her palm over so her wrist was facing up.

"'Night," she whispered.

Ryan smiled at her, a lazy smile that made her heart start thumping wildly all over again.

He brought his lips down slowly to her wrist, pressed a kiss there, then turned her hand back over. The touch of his lips, soft and pillowy, left an emotional indent on her skin.

It was one of the most intimate touches she'd ever experienced.

Ryan walked a few steps backward while she stood there. Immobile. She looked up at him and for a moment, words refused to form in her throat.

Then he took her breath away. "You know, I think you might just be better in real life than you were on paper," he said and he laughed as he turned, hand raised up over his head in a wave goodbye.

Jessica laughed until tears sprang into her eyes and she didn't miss the cheeky grin on his face as he winked before driving off. *You are, too,* she thought. *You are so much better in real life than on paper, and I never could have imagined it.*

Tonight had been crazy. Amazing.

But scary too.

Because here she was, standing on her porch, watching the taillights of his car disappear down the road, feeling like she had maybe, just maybe, fallen head over heels in love with a man who wasn't within her reach.

If they'd met under different circumstances, maybe it would have been different. But she'd promised herself time to heal, to not let anyone else in, and here she was wishing things could be different.

And Ryan didn't want this, either. He might think he did, but he didn't. Not if he knew the truth about her.

He had told her what had happened with his wife, she knew how much it had hurt him, the demons it had created that he'd never truly been able to shake. And tonight, he'd made it clear he could never cope with cancer again. Had spoken of it like the hideous disease it was.

But cancer was still as much a part of her life right now as her family was. It wasn't something she could pretend she'd never had or might never have again in the future. She was in the safe zone now, but it didn't mean it wouldn't come back or haunt her again one day. Unlikely, given the fact she'd had an elective double mastectomy, but it still worried her every day.

She knew what losing someone was like—the disease had taken her sister, too. So she couldn't blame Ryan for how he felt.

So would it be lying if she didn't tell him? If she just enjoyed his company while he was here, before he was redeployed? Would that make her a bad person, after what he'd told her tonight?

Jessica wiped tears away as they fell, heavy on her cheeks. This time she wasn't laughing. This time her tears hurt.

She wasn't going to say no to fun, but what had happened tonight hadn't just felt like fun.

It had felt like the start of something great.

Jessica heard shuffling then scratching on the other side of the door. It brought the smile back to her face.

"Hey, Herc."

She unlocked the door and picked her scruffy little boy up, holding him close to her chest. He licked at her face, tucked tightly against her body.

"Hey, baby. Come on, let's go to bed."

Hercules wriggled to get down and danced down the hall, his tiny feet padding on the carpet. He looked up at her, waiting, happy about tucking up in bed beside her.

"At least I'll always have you, huh?"

His tongue lolled out, as if he was smiling up at her.

She felt tears well at the back of her eyes again, and she didn't try to stop them. Life could be so unfair sometimes. Just when you thought you'd been through enough, coped with all you could, something else came along to steal the breath from your lungs and the fight from your soul.

CHAPTER SIX

Dear Jessica,
It's funny what you've done to me. For all this time
I've avoided coming home, and now that I want
to I don't know how long it'll be before I can. If
you believe I can make things right with my son,
then I'll give you the benefit of the doubt. Let's
hope we can sit together and laugh one day, and
you can say I told you so.

Hope you're well and that you're not sick of
writing to me yet. You've got no idea how your
letters bring a smile to this soldier's face. I haven't
had a lot to look forward to for a while, and your
letters make a world of difference.

Here's to seeing you soon.
Ryan

"Push up as hard as you can then hold."

Ryan felt his mouth twist into a grimace. This was
hard. Harder than last time, but then he was making
himself work as much as he could physically endure.

The physio pushed down on him, forcing him to exert
as much energy, as much power, as possible.

"Okay, and relax," she instructed.

He let his arm drop. The thud started again, the pain

that seemed to shoot through every inch of his skin on that side when he exercised too hard. He'd told her the pain wasn't bad because he wanted to go as hard as he could.

Maybe that hadn't been such a great idea.

Ryan wiped away the sweat that had formed on his forehead.

"You did good today."

He gave the physio what he hoped was an innocent smile. "Why don't we keep going? Another few reps?"

She shook her head, not fooled this time. "You going to tell me again that it doesn't hurt?"

Ryan reached for his workout towel and wiped it over his face. She had him there. Perhaps she'd seen through his bravado the entire time. Seen the pain in his face each time he pushed himself too far.

"I just want to get stronger again as fast as I can."

"And *I* want you to develop your strength slowly, so you can use your arm properly until you're an old man," she said tartly.

Ryan laughed. He couldn't argue with that.

"Can I ask you a personal question?"

He looked up at her. "Shoot."

"I was just wondering why you boys are always in such a hurry to get back to your unit? I get that you're all close, but isn't it nice having an excuse to be home for once?" she asked curiously.

Ryan understood what she was saying. Lots of people seemed to think that way, but they didn't get what it was like to have such an unbreakable bond with another group of men. To feel that closeness and not want to let your team down. The way he felt about his unit was indescribable. He could probably never find words to explain it.

Maybe if his wife was still alive he'd have finished up in the army already, but now...? Well, now the army was his focus, what kept him going.

"It's hard to explain," Ryan said, complying as she flexed his fingers back and stretched his muscles out. "There's something about not wanting to let your unit down, but it's also about wanting to do the right thing."

She smiled, but he didn't think she understood. Not really.

"It's not that I want to be redeployed more than being here, but I'm good at it. It's what I do best."

He was sure better at that than at being a dad.

"So you still want to get fixed up as soon as possible, right? Get back to wherever it is they want to send you."

He nodded. "Yes, ma'am."

She gave him a pat on the back. He could see she didn't truly get it, but his physio was great at her job. And truth be told, not many civilians *could* ever understand the bond and camaraderie a good soldier enjoyed with his unit.

"Same time on Tuesday. And don't leave here until you've stretched out some more."

Ryan watched as she walked away. He sat there, thinking, barely noticing the other people in the room.

He always felt so useless, so powerless when he was here, even though he knew he was making good progress. Because it didn't matter how hard he tried, he was never as strong as he wanted to be.

Ryan took a deep, long gulp of water before moving

to stretch out his muscles some more. He knew he'd be sore in the morning if he didn't do as she'd said.

He couldn't help but think that the only time lately he hadn't thought about his weakness, about what was holding him back physically, was when he'd been with Jessica. Last night he hadn't thought about his arm once. Even when it had ached as he'd lifted it to touch her face, the pain had been nothing.

Or nothing compared to not letting his skin brush against hers.

He liked that she made him smile. That she listened to him.

That she blushed every time they were close, or the way a smile hinted at the corners of her mouth when he spoke.

For a guy who had sworn to never let another woman close again he sure could have fooled himself. Because when he was with Jessica, close to her, beside her, there was no other place he wanted to be. He couldn't offer her a future, anything more than a friendship or short-term relationship really, but he'd been honest with her. He was only back for a short time. No matter how much he liked her, his duty was to his unit, and he would be back serving again as soon as he passed the physical.

Maybe one day in the future they could be something more, but right now he didn't know what his long-term future held. His timing was way off, but he wasn't going to let that stop him seeing her now.

If only he could repair his relationship with his son, he'd feel like he was making real progress being back here.

He stood and tried to ignore the pain as it twinged through his biceps.

Ryan smiled. He might have said no to the pain

medication his doctor had prescribed, but Jessica was purely organic and the best pain relief he could wish for. He dialed her number. He didn't care if asking her out again tonight was too soon. He wanted to see her and it wasn't like he had all the time in the world.

If she was up for some fun while he was here, then he wanted to spend as much time with her as he could. Whether that was just hanging out together or something more.

Jessica stretched back and closed her eyes. The sun felt good on her skin. Like it was soaking through her pores to warm her from the inside out.

Hercules's bark made her open her eyes. He was chasing Bella's daughter, Ruby, around the yard, running alongside her and bouncing up and down.

Jess laughed. "Better than any toy, right?"

Bella agreed. "Nothing makes her giggle like that dog of yours."

"You know it's funny, but I don't think I could ever tire of hearing that little girl laugh."

They both sat back to watch the game between dog and child.

Bella was like her sister. When her own sister had died, Bella had been there for her, unwavering in her support even though it had been a lot for another teenager to cope with. And now Jessica liked to be there for Ruby. It was her way of paying Bella back for all she'd done. In the past and when Jess had been sick, too. Bella had never let her down.

Jessica watched as her brother, Steven, pushed himself up off the grass and stretched out his legs. He'd been lying back, swigging on a beer with Bella's husband, but she figured the barbeque was calling him.

"Are Mom and Dad coming over?"

Steven dropped a kiss to her head as he passed. "Nope. They had some old-folks thing to go to."

They all laughed at him.

"They're not that old."

Steven shrugged. "When you choose bingo over a real night out, you're getting old."

Jessica made a noise in her throat but she could hardly reprimand him. Aside from the fact he was her older brother, Steven didn't mean a word of it. He loved their parents as much as she did.

"You wouldn't get me a beer would you?" he asked.

This time she stood up and thumped him on the arm. "If you weren't so charming I'd tell you to get it yourself."

Steven pouted and made them all laugh again. "Then who'd make you burgers?"

Jess stood up and walked inside. She liked it here. Steven's place was a bachelor pad, not exactly warm and cosy like her house, but it always felt good. They'd had plenty of good times here, fun times with friends and their little family. It was like her second home.

Jessica reached into the fridge for a six-pack of beer just as her phone rang, vibrating and singing in her jeans pocket.

"Ouch!" She hit her head and almost dropped the beer. Darn phone, she thought. "Hello?"

The voice on the other end made her close the fridge and lean against it.

"Hey, Jess, it's Ryan."

She took a moment to catch her breath. Ryan. How could the sound of his voice make her legs wobble like that? Her heart was pounding.

"Hey."

"I was wondering if you were free tonight?"

Heck. She could hardly bail on her brother and Bella, not when they'd been planning to all catch up together for weeks.

But an offer from Ryan was sure tempting.

"Ah, I'm actually out already. At a barbeque."

There was a beat of silence.

"Oh sure, no problem. Maybe another time."

Jess cringed. She didn't want to say no to him. Well, she did and she didn't, she couldn't decide, but right now saying no felt like the wrong answer. Especially after that kiss last night.

She sighed. *Kisses* plural, more like.

"Ryan, I..."

Jessica looked out the window at her brother goofing around, chasing her dog. Bella was sitting on her husband's knee, laughing as her daughter bounced up and down with excitement as she played.

Would it be so bad if she asked Ryan over?

"It's fine, really, we can just catch up some other time."

"No, I mean, why don't you come join me? It's only a few of us. Just casual," she said.

He went silent again. Jessica pressed her ear closer to the phone, harder, willing him to say yes and terrified at the same time.

"Are you sure? I don't want to intrude."

"I'd love to see you again. We're sitting around having a beer and waiting for my—" Jess paused and watched Steven entertain Ruby "—idiot brother to get started with the meat patties."

"I'll see you soon then."

Jessica gave him directions then hung up. She leaned

against the fridge again and tried to steady her thoughts. Had she done the right thing?

Probably not, but she was desperate to see him again. To be near him, to touch him and see whether she'd imagined what had happened yesterday. To see if maybe the connection hadn't been as strong as she'd remembered it to be.

Or whether it was even stronger.

To see whether he was worth the heartache that was sure to come when he left again in a couple of months' time. Because no matter how much she told herself she was okay with his leaving, she'd never allowed herself to get close to a man before without thinking there was a chance at some sort of future.

"You making the beer yourself, sis?"

Steven's call forced her to move her feet, reach back in for the beers and go outside.

He gave her a puzzled look when she walked out again. He dropped his cooking utensil and moved toward her but she put up her hand.

"I'm fine."

He was overprotective. Always worrying about her, especially after the cancer. But he'd already lost one sister, she could hardly blame him for wanting to keep her safe.

"You look like you've seen a ghost."

She waved her hand in the air and tried to relax. "I was just chatting to a friend on the phone." Jess gave Bella a sharp look, but her friend was already smiling. She had guessed exactly whom she'd been talking to.

"Oh." Steven looked unsure but he turned back to the meat.

"He's, ah, going to come over and join us soon, actually."

"He?" Steven growled.

Now Steven was holding his cooking utensil at a scary angle, like he was about to behead someone with it.

Jess gulped. She should have predicted this. "Yes, *he*," she repeated, standing up to her brother. "I think I mentioned that I had a pen pal, a soldier who I wrote to."

The look on Steven's face spelt thunder. There was a possibility he could have summoned a hurricane just with his expression. "And he's coming here? *Now?*"

"He's a friend, Steven, nothing to get concerned about."

He grimaced then turned away from her. Bella was wriggling in her chair, but Jess shook her head. She didn't want this to become a big deal. Right now Ryan *was* just a friend, and the last thing she needed was Steven getting worked up over it.

"His name is Ryan, and he's back for a while to recover. He had surgery and as soon as he's better he'll be back with his unit, so there is *absolutely no reason* to overreact. It's not like he's even here for long," she told him.

Steven shrugged, but he didn't turn around. She could tell he wasn't happy about it. But then given her recent track record, she could hardly blame him.

"And I don't want him knowing about the cancer."

That made him turn. Now he looked like Neptune about to command the entire ocean. "What kind of friend do you have to keep your cancer from?"

She reached for the bottle opener and popped the top off a beer for Steven. She passed it to him.

"The kind of friend who doesn't need to know. Okay?"

He took the beer and tipped it up, draining a third of the bottle. "If he hurts you, I'll deck him."

She had no doubt that he'd try. Her only issue was that even with a less than perfect arm, Ryan could probably kill her brother with his bare hands.

Bella waved her over and Jess went to sit beside her.

"He only wants to protect you," Bella said quietly.

Jess knew that, she did. And she liked that he was always there for her. After what her ex had done to her, she couldn't blame her brother. She'd been left heart-broken, facing surgery and serious chemotherapy on her own. One moment she'd been looking forward to a wedding, and the next she'd been fighting for her life without the man she'd once loved by her side.

Ryan was different though. He'd been there for his wife, by her side, and she'd lost her battle. He might not want to go back to that dark place ever again, but it wasn't something she could fault him for. He was a different kind of man. Honorable. Dependable.

"Is it so bad that I don't want him to know?" she asked Bella in a low voice.

Her friend squeezed her hand and shook her head. "No. No, it's not."

"He's not going to be around long enough for it to matter, right?"

Bella sighed then shrugged. She didn't answer; it was a hypothetical question, anyway.

"You were right yesterday," Jessica told her. "It's time I let my hair down, enjoyed being in remission, being alive, and being in the company of a man." She took a tiny sip of beer and tucked her feet up under her on the chair. She liked Ryan. She didn't have to pretend otherwise. So why was she still trying to convince herself he was just another friend?

Because after what had happened last night, she knew that they were way beyond friends now.

Ryan pushed the button on his key to lock the car and walked toward the house. It was stupid, being nervous about meeting Jessica's friends, but it had been a long time since he'd done normal stuff like this.

And his latest argument with George was playing on his mind. Hard to ignore.

His son had finally found his tongue, but the words coming out weren't pretty. Ryan grimaced. Maybe George did genuinely hate him. And if he did, what on earth was he going to do about it?

He knocked at the door, sternly pushing back thoughts of his son. It swung back and Jessica grinned at him from inside.

"Hey, Ryan."

The warmth that spread through him, the smile he couldn't help but give her in return, somehow took away all the pain.

She was like his ray of sunshine on the gloomiest of days.

"Hi," he answered.

She beckoned with her hand. "Come on in."

Ryan hesitated for a second too long. He should have kissed her on the cheek, touched his hand to her arm, anything. But he'd waited too long. Now it would just be awkward. It was the second time he'd managed to do that and he vowed not to miss his chance again.

"So this is a friend's place?"

She shook her head. "My brother's."

Oh, dear. He'd walked in on a family do or something.

When she'd said her brother was on burger duty he hadn't realized it was his house.

"I don't want to intrude, if you're doing the whole family thing."

She laughed and tucked a strand of hair behind her ear, her expression shy. "It's just my brother and another couple of friends."

"If you're sure."

This time she was braver in reassuring him. This time she reached out and touched his arm, so lightly he could have missed it if he wasn't watching the way her skin connected with his.

"It's really nice to see you again."

Ryan felt the warmth spread through him, just like it had when he'd arrived. He'd thought of little else but her since last night, except for when he was trying to deal with his son, and being with her again, right now, sure seemed right.

But then maybe he'd been away so long he wasn't sure what he was feeling anymore.

"Come and meet everyone," she urged.

Ryan stepped out into the yard and looked up. But the smile fell from his face in an instant, leaving him cold. That warmth that had spread through him like cookies just taken from the oven died like ice had been poured on them.

It wasn't hard to pick out her brother. He was the one looking like he'd crush every bone in Ryan's body, given half a chance. He stood up straighter, lifted his chin. He understood protective. If he had a sister like Jessica he'd probably be the same. But she was a grown woman and she'd invited him over. And he wasn't the kind of guy easily intimidated—even if he did respect the big-brother macho act.

"Ryan, this is my friend Bella, and her husband, Bruce," Jess said, making the introductions.

Ryan turned his attention to the petite blonde sitting with a little girl on her lap. Her double-wattage smile made up for the deathlike stare of the brother. He took the few steps to shake her husband's hand.

"And little Ruby, of course."

He smiled at the pudgy-armed child wriggling to get down.

Jessica moved closer to Ryan when she turned to face her brother.

"And this is my big brother, Steve." He felt her stiffen as Steve walked over. "I promise he won't bite."

Ryan extended his hand and regretted it the moment the other man clasped it. His grip was tight, viselike, and his dodgy arm was barely up to matching his strength.

He tried not to scowl as pain shot up his arm. He was used to being the strongest, never losing an arm wrestle. Ryan clamped down his jaw and took the pain, refused to give in to it. Didn't let it show even though he was burning inside.

"Nice to meet you, Steve."

Jessica smiled sweetly in Ryan's direction before taking a step closer to her brother and kicking him in the shin.

"Ow!" Steve dropped his iron grip and stepped back.

"He can be a pain in the backside." Jessica smiled as her brother glared at her then went back to the barbeque. "It's not until we have company over that we realize how barbaric he really is."

Ryan smiled, but it was hard. His arm hurt like hell,

scorching hot. He hated the ache that was thumping under his skin.

"So, Ryan, Jess tells us you've not long been back."

He took the beer Jessica passed him and sat down in the nearest seat, looking over at her friend as she spoke.

"I'm home for a bit of rest and recovery, then hopefully back with my unit."

Jessica sat down on the grass nearby. He moved to stand, to give her his seat, but she shook her head and crossed her legs, Hercules tucking in beside her.

It was hard not to watch her. Not to ignore everyone else and just drink her in. The way her ponytail fell over one shoulder, her tanned skin soft against the white of her T-shirt. The scoop neck showed him just enough cleavage to make it hard to swallow his beer.

And that smile. The way she cast her eyes downward when her lips curved up. It made him wonder what he'd ever done to have that look directed his way. To deserve her attention.

"So you're not tempted to stay here, now you're home?"

Ryan forced his eyes from Jessica and focused his attention back on her friends. "Tempting, but no." He watched as Jessica played with a blade of grass, not looking up. "I need to be back with my unit."

Steve appeared next to him then. "So you're definitely leaving?"

Ryan nodded. Had he not made that clear?

Her brother gave Ryan what he guessed was a smile. It should have been easy to tell but it wasn't. Unsaid words hung between them. Was Steve wondering why he was bothering with Jess, because he was leaving?

"How are those burgers coming along?" Jessica asked, breaking the silence.

Steve turned back to the meat, putting his hands up like he was surrendering.

Ryan took another swig of beer.

Maybe staying home with George would have been easier than facing off with the brother.

Jessica went out to Ryan's car with him. It had been an interesting evening.

The fact it was only nine and the night was over told her it probably hadn't been that successful. But then she'd pushed her luck hoping it would be.

It had reinforced a few things in her mind, though.

Her brother was an idiot sometimes, but he loved her and did his best to protect her. Even if it annoyed her intensely sometimes, she got it.

The other thing she'd learned was that Ryan was the kind of guy she wished she'd met years ago. Instead of wasting all her time on her idiot ex. Ryan had stood up to her brother with ease, and he was up-front and honest.

Bella had been right. What harm was there in having a little fun with a nice guy, when there was no chance of having her heart broken or breaking his? If he was only here for a short time, they could have a blast, enjoy one another and say goodbye as friends.

They were only a few steps from his car.

Jessica willed her body to cooperate and took a deep breath. She fell back one step and reached for Ryan's hand, catching his wrist then letting her fingers glide down to his palm as he turned.

"Ryan, stop."

She registered the surprise in his eyes as he faced her, but she didn't let herself think about it. She'd been

waiting to do this all night, wishing she had the courage.
Jess kept hold of his hand and pulled him closer. His
body obliged. Then she reached her other hand to cup
his cheek, standing on tiptoe to kiss him.

"Jessica…" he murmured against her mouth.

She shook her head. "Just kiss me."

His lips met hers as if they'd been made to touch.
But he only let her feather-light kiss brush him for a
moment before he pushed closer to her, deepened their
embrace and slipped his hand around her waist, pressing
her gently against him.

His hold was tender but his kisses became more insistent, his mouth moving firmly over hers, his breath hot
against her skin when he pulled away, before crushing
her lips against his again.

Jessica sighed into his mouth, head cloudy, as if she
was being swept away on a wave of happiness, float-
ing with the tenderness of his touch and the way he'd
responded to her.

"I'm not usually brave enough to do things like that,"
she whispered.

Ryan smiled down at her, touched his forehead to
hers, still holding her, both his arms around her waist
now. He raised a hand and oh, so gently let his fingers
skim her face, caress her cheek.

"Well lucky me then, huh?"

When she smiled at him, her lower lip caught between
her teeth, he spun her around, one arm tight around her
back, then pressed her against the car. Almost rough,
but she knew he wouldn't hurt her. That he wouldn't
even think one bruise on her skin was acceptable. And
then he was kissing her again. This time harder, more
urgently.

Jess let her head dip back as he pressed into her, his

body hard against hers, fitted snugly against her shape. She moaned as he left her lips and traced a row of kisses down her neck, stopping with the last touch against the indent of her collarbone.

When he raised his eyes again, held her face with both his hands, she couldn't help but giggle. A tiny gurgling noise that rose in her throat.

"What's so funny?" he asked.

She smiled then sighed, letting her lower body press into his, as he moved his upper body back slightly to accommodate her.

"It's just…"

He nodded. "I know."

She wondered if he did. If he understood how conflicted she felt.

And still they stood there, bodies locked together.

"Can I make it up to you and cook you dinner this weekend?"

Ryan raised an eyebrow. "I must be missing something here."

"What?"

He dropped a kiss to her nose then took a step back. Jess shivered. She hadn't been ready to let any air between them yet, could have stood like that all night. Against his rock-hard, strong body, and melted against that soft, pillowy mouth of his all evening.

"What do you need to make up to me?" he asked.

"For the way my brother was. The way tonight turned out."

He caught her hand and traced a finger across her palm. "Believe me, sweetheart, you more than made up for his frostiness."

Jessica's entire body felt hot, clammy. She wasn't used to being so bold, and she certainly wasn't used to talking about her actions. "He's, well, protective over me. We lost my sister a few years back, and he's made it his personal mission to keep me safe."

She wasn't lying. The fact they'd lost their sister had made Steven protective. Her ending up with the same cancer had made him worse, spurred his "big bad wolf" routine into action, but keeping that part from Ryan wasn't the same as not telling the truth.

"I've met my share of tough guys, Jess, and your brother doesn't strike me as anything other than worried about his little sister making a bad choice. He just wants to keep you safe, right?"

She liked the kindness on Ryan's face, the way he looked so open. It was not how she'd expected him to be. The soldier who'd seemed so tortured on paper was surprisingly unmessed-up in real life. Or else he was just really good at disguising it.

"I still want to make it up to you."

He grinned. "I'd like that."

Jessica didn't know where to look. His eyes were shining at her, suggesting things she wasn't sure about. Things she might want but maybe wasn't ready for. Yet.

"So dinner Sunday night?" she offered.

"Yeah." Ryan squeezed her hand and opened his door. "Maybe you could tell me about your sister."

Jess felt a shiver trawl her spine, her pulse suddenly thumping. She didn't want to go there. Didn't want to tell him how her sister had died, without being able to admit what she'd been through.

It was too close. Still too real for her to open up to him. And if she told him the truth, about her sister dying and then her getting the same disease, he would know she'd been lying all this time. That she'd listened to him talk about his wife, listened to him say he didn't ever want to be in that position again, and pretended she was fine. When she hadn't been fine, and still might not be.

"Maybe."

He didn't seem put out. Relief washed through her as he casually shrugged. "I'll see you Sunday."

She pushed his car door shut when he put down the window.

"Sunday," she affirmed.

Ryan pulled away slowly from the curb.

She watched him for a moment, then walked back to the house. Even though she felt a little guilty, that she should have just told him from the very beginning what had happened to her last year, about the breast cancer, it was so nice that he didn't know.

Would he hold her the same if he knew? Or would he think her as breakable as a tiny bird? Would he want her so bad if he knew what she'd been through? Especially when his wife had battled something similar and lost. From what he'd so honestly told her, she already knew the answer to that.

Jessica looked up and found Steve leaning in the door frame, his body filling the space. She glared at him.

"How long have you been standing there?"

He shrugged, not even caring he'd been found out, that she'd caught him as good as spying on her. "Long enough."

She gave him a shove in the shoulder and walked past him.

Once upon a time he would have shoved her back, grabbed her and made her beg for mercy, the way they'd been as kids, play fighting at every opportunity.

Tonight he just shut the door and followed. "You really like this guy, don't you?"

"He's only here for a couple of months."

He grabbed her shoulder, his fingers firm enough to stop her. She didn't turn.

"That wasn't my question."

Jess spun around. "So what? So what if I do?"

His eyes crumpled, the creases at the side of his eyes, the ones that hadn't been there before she'd battled her cancer, appearing. Jessica hated seeing the way he'd aged.

She relaxed against his touch. "I'm sorry, I didn't mean to snap at you. I've just got a lot on my mind."

"I was going to say that he actually seemed like a nice guy."

Jessica let out a shuddering breath. "He is."

"And I can tell he likes you."

She closed her eyes, embarrassed. Had Steve seen the way she'd kissed him? "But...?"

"But he's going away soon and I don't want you to get hurt."

Argh. There he went again. Just when she was starting to think he wasn't going to interfere. But he was only telling her what she already knew.

"I know what I'm getting myself into, Steve."

She turned to walk away again, but his words made her stop.

"But does *he?*" Her brother paused. She could feel him behind her but he didn't touch her this time, didn't try to stop her from walking away. "You need to tell him, Jess. He needs to know."

Tears filled her eyes then, but she forced down the choke in her throat. Wouldn't let it take hold of her. "Or what?"

His voice softened. "I just don't want to see you get hurt, okay?"

Too late for that. Her heart had already been broken before, shattered into so many pieces she'd wondered if it could ever recover. She was in no danger of Ryan doing that to her.

"I don't want him to treat me any different, Steve. I just want him to like me for me."

Steve moved closer, touched both his hands to her shoulders, waiting until she spun around to face him. "He'll still want you, Jess. If he's half-decent it won't scare him, but you need to tell him."

"I can't," she whispered.

Steve couldn't understand, because she didn't want to tell him the whole story. The truth about Ryan's wife's death. And it wasn't her story to tell anyway.

"Come here." Steve pulled her into his embrace and held her as she cried. As the tears soaked the shoulder of his T-shirt.

He might be an ass sometimes, an overprotective oaf, but when she needed him he was always there for her. She leaned heavily against him, safe in his arms.

"He's not Mark, you know," he told her, holding her tight. "The way he looked at you tonight, the way he was around you, I can just tell."

She nodded against his shoulder and closed her eyes until the tears stopped.

"What if I want to be the old me for a little while? What if I want to enjoy his company and have fun while he's here? Does he really need to know?" she begged.

Steve stepped back. "You're not that kind of girl, Jess. If you were, your ex leaving you wouldn't have hit you so hard."

It was true. She'd never been interested in casual

relationships, but this was different. This was getting outside her comfort zone with a man who wasn't making her any promises, who was only here for a short time. Was it so bad that she wanted to be with him while she could?

"I don't want him to know, Steve. It's more complicated than I can explain."

"I'm not saying anything if you're not. It's your choice."

She kissed her brother on the cheek. "So if you liked him so much why were you so hard on him?"

That made him grin. "I had to test him. No point letting him off easy."

Jessica rolled her eyes. "You're terrible."

He linked arms with her and they walked back into the kitchen. "Nope, I'm your big brother. And it means I'm allowed to be the tough guy."

As much as she moaned about him, there sure was something nice about knowing she had Steve around to protect her.

Ryan sat on his bed and toyed with his dog tag. It comforted him, the weight of it, reminded him of all those nights he'd lain awake on the other side of the world. Thinking about what he'd done, what he should have done and what the future held.

Part of him was itching to be back with his unit, but the other part was feeling settled. Happy to be back home on American soil.

And spending time with a girl he was going crazy about.

But it wasn't helping him with his son. Jessica had helped him, plenty, but his feelings for her weren't making things right with George. Instead he was showing her the person he wanted to be without proving the same to his son.

Something was weird about being back under the same roof as his parents. About having his son down the hall yet not feeling brave enough to go into his room to try to talk to him.

When he'd gone back to war after his wife died, he hadn't had a choice. He had been granted emergency leave when she'd been diagnosed, and the army had been understanding when he'd kept extending it. But the reality was that he'd owed them more time, and even though it had been hard going away again after all that had happened, he'd done it.

Back then, he'd told his parents they could move into his house, to keep things less traumatic for George. Besides, their place had been small, and the home Ryan had shared with his wife was comfortable and much bigger.

Ryan had felt like his paying the mortgage, making sure his parents and son were financially okay, was enough. But it hadn't been enough and until a couple of weeks ago he hadn't truly understood that.

Jessica was helping him to clear his head. To realize what it meant to be a real father again. Somehow her letters and her compassion, the way she made him feel when they were together, were reminding him of the man he'd once been.

Because right now the man he was around her wasn't the same man he was around his son.

And it was fear holding him back. Because when his son refused to talk to him, he wasn't telling him he hated him. Ryan could still pretend that one day things might be okay again.

But unless he did something about it, he might lose his chance forever.

He smiled as he thought about Jessica. About the way she'd fallen into his arms tonight and kissed him like he'd almost forgotten how to. It had been a long time since he'd held a woman, and with her he felt like himself again.

It spurred him into action. If he was going to be that guy, he had to be him in every aspect of his life. And that meant making things right with George.

Now.

No more excuses.

He got up and opened the door, then walked down the hall. Light was still spilling out from beneath his son's door, even though it was late.

Ryan knocked softly. There was no response, so he opened it.

George was lying on his bed, earphones in his ears, iPod resting on his chest. The lamp was still on, even though he'd fallen asleep.

He stood there, towering over his boy as he slept. His face was so young in slumber. There was no trace of the sulky preteen, almost a hint of the face he'd known years ago, when they'd been so close.

Ryan bent to pick up the iPod and gently reached to take the earphones out.

George stirred. Then opened his eyes.

Ryan froze.

His son went to say something, went to move, but Ryan put his hand against George's chest and slowly bent his legs until he could sit on the bed. George didn't say a word.

There were questions in his son's eyes. Questions he

wished would come out in the open so he could tell him the truth, could tell him how sorry he was.

George pulled the cord so his ears were free. Then glared at him. Ryan went to move, to stand up again, but his son grabbed his hand. Made him stop. Then George burst into tears, his entire body shaking from the sobs deep in his chest.

"Come here." Ryan took his boy into his arms and held him, held him so tight he hoped he wasn't hurting him, and fought the emotions that were running through his own body, thrumming through him, desperate to escape. His eyes were burning, body tense as he held his son, the boy suddenly feeling so young and vulnerable in his arms. "Shhh, it's okay."

"You left me," George managed to say between sobs. "Why did you leave me?"

"I'm sorry," he said, holding him even tighter, never wanting to let him go. "I'm so, so sorry."

"Grams told me," George sobbed, "she said you would be leaving again soon."

Ryan squeezed his eyes shut and did his best to force away his own tears, to push them away and be strong for his son. It was like his heart was being pulled from his body to beat in the unforgiving heat of the desert sun. Left to wither, exposed to the world.

"I'll never leave you like that again, ever." Ryan said the words into his son's hair. "I promise."

"But you are going back?"

George pushed away from him to sit upright. His eyes full of hurt, questioning his father.

"I am going back," he said, knowing he had to be honest. There was no point in pretending otherwise. But it was also time for him to be honest with himself. He wasn't done with the army, not yet, and he'd already agreed to another term. But it was time to prioritize, and he'd given his country years of service. Had been a dedicated and loyal soldier.

Now maybe it was time to put that same amount of energy into being the father he'd once been. The father he'd always wanted to be. Maybe it wasn't just about his duty to the army anymore.

"This time will be my last tour," he said, knowing he was speaking the truth, even though he'd never decided, until right now, that it was going to be his final stint away. "I will go away one more time, then I'll be done. And this time I'll be there for you even though I'm away—we'll stay in touch properly, okay?"

George looked unsure, hesitant, but Ryan didn't care. Tonight had been a major breakthrough. And all it had taken was some courage on his behalf to take the first step. His son might not believe his words yet, but Ryan would see his promise through and show his son he could be trusted. It was up to him to give George a reason to trust in him.

"You promise?"

He nodded and pulled his boy in for another hug. "I promise, kid. I'm not going to let you down again."

George held him back hard, clinging on to his father, and Ryan sent a silent prayer skyward. He wouldn't trade anything for this moment. The pain in his arm, the hurt of his memories, nothing would be worth sacrificing for knowing his son was close. For feeling like forgiveness was possible.

For remembering what it was like to be a real dad again.

CHAPTER SEVEN

~~Dear Ryan,~~
~~I guess you might be wondering just how I un-~~
~~derstand what you've gone through. Maybe you~~
~~haven't thought about it, but I feel like we're close~~
~~enough now that I need to tell you something—~~
~~that I've gone through what you have. Lost some-~~
~~one close. Battled with my own health and my own~~
~~demons. That I've had...~~

JESSICA SAT OUTSIDE, one hand raised to shield her eyes from the sun. Hercules lay at her feet, her constant companion. She ran the toes of one foot across his fur, the touch comforting her.

She couldn't stop thinking about the letter she'd almost sent Ryan. The one in which she'd tried to tell him everything. The one that was her opening her heart and telling him what had happened in her past, and what she was scared might happen in her future.

But then she'd scrunched it up into a ball and thrown it out. Forgotten about it. Except for last night, when the words of that letter had played over and over in her mind. She hadn't even realized they'd be in her memory bank still, but they had been. Every single word. Keeping sleep from her and haunting her thoughts.

Maybe her brother was right. Maybe she should tell Ryan. Maybe it was the right thing to do.

But she wasn't going to. If she did, she'd have to end their romance. Right now. Or more likely he'd end it straight away before she had the chance.

If she didn't? They could continue on, enjoying themselves, and Ryan could go back to his unit oblivious to what she'd been through. And why should he know? He had enough of his own problems to deal with.

Jess stood and stretched. She needed to get back into her studio and paint, unwind and enjoy her creativity. There was no use worrying over something once you'd made a decision, and she had.

It didn't matter how many times she went over it.

Ryan wasn't going to find out, she wasn't going to tell him, and that was the end of it.

"Come on, mister."

Hercules yawned and padded after her.

They had Bella coming around to visit this afternoon, and she'd be able to talk the subject to death if she wanted. Right now, it was time to paint.

And there was going to be no thinking about the past or the future. It was about time she learned to live in the now.

Ryan knew he had Jess to thank for reconnecting with his son. They had a long way to go, but they'd made progress. When he'd left George's room last night, he'd felt lighter somehow, like the burden he'd carried all this time had been a weight on his shoulders, pushing him down, trying to cripple him.

Even his arm felt better, despite the pummelling it had taken last night when Jess's brother had nearly crushed his hand.

But it was all worth it. Having George on speaking terms with him again, listening to his son talk and watching him smile, it was the best reward he could ever have wished for.

And all it had taken was a little courage.

"You want to walk down for an ice cream or something?"

George looked up and put down the video game control. "Yeah, okay."

He was going to have to get used to those kind of responses. Kids didn't seem that enthusiastic over anything these days. But he wasn't complaining. Not while his son was actually talking to him.

"Let's go."

They stood up to leave. George walked close to him, but Ryan resisted the urge to sling his arm around his son's shoulder. They might have made progress, but it was going to be slow and he didn't want to push it.

Jessica sat at the café, Hercules's lead around her ankle. She couldn't stop laughing at Bella. Her friend was in a particularly entertaining mood. Even though Bella had left her daughter at home with her husband, she was all they talked about, and it made Jess feel good.

"You know, Mr. Soldier Stud and you would make beautiful babies, if I do say so myself."

Jess almost spat out her mouthful of coffee. "Babies?"

How had the subject swung around to her all of a sudden?

"Oh, come on," Bella said as she swatted her hand through the air. "Don't go telling me you don't want a family of your own one day."

Her heart seemed to twinge, like a small knife had

been thrown into it. She had always dreamed of being
a mother, but the chance of that happening seemed less
and less likely these days. It wasn't even the kind of
thing she'd let herself think about this last year.

"Maybe, Bella, but not with Ryan."

Her friend snorted. "Why not Ryan? He's gorgeous,
funny, buff, did I mention gorgeous?"

It wasn't like Jess didn't agree, but it just wasn't a
possibility. "You forget that he's a widower, a father,
and oh, that's right. A soldier. Who's returning to his
unit soon."

"Okay, so I get the soldier part, but that's doable.
Heaps of soldiers are great husbands." Bella paused.
"The fact that he's a widower doesn't mean he can't fall
in love again, and so what if he already has a son?"

"I know it sounds lame, but…"

There was no way Ryan would consider a relationship with her if he knew the truth, and she didn't want
to get serious. She wasn't ready to trust someone like
that again. To put all her love and dreams into another
person only to have them sucked away forever. And
she didn't intend on putting anyone through her getting
sick again. It was unlikely, but not impossible, and she'd
rather be alone until she at least hit the five-year remission mark.

Bella gestured at her to continue.

"It's nothing. Let's just talk about something else,
okay?"

Her friend just laughed. Not the response she'd
expected.

"Well, well. Look who's walking toward us."

Jess glanced up and didn't see anyone. "Where?"

"Over your shoulder." Bella smirked. "It's the stud
himself."

Jessica scowled at Bella before turning. "You seriously need to get out more. You're getting tragic."

But she felt her own heart start to race—the flutter in her belly that started whenever she was around Ryan began tickling her over and over.

Ryan hadn't seen them. He was walking with a young boy, clearly his son, and they were talking. Talking!

The nervousness she'd felt at him walking toward her disappeared as she watched the two of them smiling and chatting. Something major must have happened last night.

He'd be over the moon to be spending time with George.

Jessica felt her cheeks ignite. She hoped the smile on his face still had something to do with their kiss, too. It sure had her heart racing again just thinking about it.

Bella kicked her under the table. "Well? Get up!"

She glared at Bella before rising. She raised one hand, hesitantly. An even wider smile crossed Ryan's face when he saw her. She watched as he touched his son on the shoulder and directed him their way.

"Hi, Ryan," Jessica called out as they came nearer, swallowing away her nervousness.

"Hi." He gave her a beamer of a smile back and put his hand back on the boy's shoulder. "Jess, I'd like you to meet my son, George."

The kid gave her an awkward smile. "Hey."

"Hi, George. I've heard so much about you."

"And this is Bella," Ryan said, gesturing toward her friend.

George nodded in Bella's direction.

"So where are you two off to?"

Ryan stepped back slightly from his son. She wanted to reach out and touch him, to reassure him that he was doing a good job, but she didn't dare move any closer. They were only friends, and his son didn't need any confusing messages sent his way. Not when he was finally on speaking terms with his father.

"We're going to grab an ice cream then walk back home."

She was dying to know what had happened. "Sounds like a plan. I'd invite you to join us but you two probably want to spend some time alone together, right?"

George was shuffling his feet, head down, awkward. She felt sorry for him.

"Yeah," said Ryan, obviously picking up on his son's discomfort. "We had better get going."

That made George look up.

"Nice to see you, Ryan," Jess said.

"Yeah, you, too. See you, Bella."

Bella waved and grinned back at him.

"Great to meet you, George. Have a nice afternoon," Jess said.

The boy met Jessica's gaze, and she wasn't sure what she saw there. A touch of happiness perhaps, but more uncertainty than anything. She wished she could help him, talk to him maybe, but Ryan would find his way with him. It looked like they'd made some good progress. And it wasn't about how they got there, it was about how well they connected along the way. Ryan was his father and no matter how hard he was finding it, George was his son and deep down he would want to let his dad in. No child wanted to feel alone.

They started to walk away, father and son, before Ryan turned back. His large frame against George's slight one brought a smile to her face all over again.

"We still on for tomorrow night?"

Jess nodded. "I'll see you around seven."

Ryan gave her a wink and turned away again, but she hardly noticed it. It didn't make her heart palpitate like it usually would. Because it was George's last look at her over his shoulder that registered in her brain. The look of horror that passed through his eyes, the disbelief, said it all.

She wanted to run after them, explain she was only friends with his dad, tell Ryan that he needed to talk to his son about them. But it was too late.

She could have been wrong, but from the extra distance now between them, and the despairing stoop of George's shoulders, she knew she was right.

He had gone from happy to be out with his father to wondering if his dad was trying to replace his mom. And if he thought Ryan had come home for her and not for him, his son, then they'd end up right back at square one all over again.

"You all right?"

Bella pulled her back to reality.

"Why does everything have to be so complicated?" Jess asked.

Hercules moaned at her feet, a big sigh that made her wish she could do the same, whinge then put her paws over her eyes to block out the world.

Bella had no idea what she was talking about, and Jessica didn't want to discuss it. The last thing she needed was something else to panic about.

"Tell me more about Ruby, okay? Just make me smile."

Bella frowned but didn't push the point. Sometimes even her best friend knew when not to pry.

Ryan was starting to feel like there was a pattern developing as he drove toward Jessica's house. His palms had started to clam up and he was getting nervous again. Not alarmingly nervous, but it was there, and it wasn't something he was used to feeling.

Today had been good, and yesterday had been even better. George had gone a little quiet on him after they'd bumped into Jess, but they'd had fun, hung out and started to get to know one another again.

And now he had something else to look forward to. An entire evening with Jess, at her place.

He grinned to himself as he drove. Even though he had his arm resting on the open window ledge, and it was throbbing with a hint of pain, he didn't care. There were too many good things going on his life to worry about something he had no control over. His physio had told him he was progressing well, there were no indications of it being a long-term problem, not after the surgery going so well, and he just needed to keep up his exercises.

So having fun with his son, and with a woman like Jessica, was something he could enjoy before he had to go back to work. As hard as it would be to return this time, he was looking forward to being with the guys again, and now that he'd decided it would be his last tour, he had to make the most of being back with his unit.

Ryan pulled onto her street.

He didn't know what exactly it was about her, but something about spending time with Jessica felt so right. After his wife had died, he'd never wanted to be close to another woman again. Never wanted to feel so helpless again, so weak. And until recently he'd thought he'd feel like that for the rest of his life.

But Jessica was quickly changing his feelings. He didn't know what she wanted, if she felt the same way as he did, but this was starting to feel real. Part of him wanted to take it slow, to stay as friends yet something more, but then he also wanted to make things happen more quickly. To make the most of his time back home and see if something special could happen between them.

Because in the span of a week, Jessica had gone from pen pal and good friend, to meaning a whole lot more to him than any other woman had since his wife.

And he liked it. Liked the way she made him feel, the effect she had on him. Whether she felt the same was another matter entirely, but from the way she'd kissed him the other night, he liked to think he could hope.

More than hope.

He liked to think he was in with a real chance.

If he was going to be coming back for good soon, then maybe that meant a chance at a future together.

Jessica fluffed around in the kitchen, knowing she had no purpose, yet not being able to stop herself from moving. It was just a casual dinner at her place, not exactly some grand dinner party, but she was like a ball of wool writhing to untangle. On edge.

She'd put together a simple pasta dish, lots of fresh ingredients tossed with olive oil and lemon juice in a pan, so there was hardly anything culinary to worry about. And dessert was a cake she'd made earlier in the day, but she still felt panicky.

The knock at the door came while she was eyeing up her glass of wine and deciding whether or not to drain it for courage. She was leaning on the counter, staring at it.

Jessica turned away from the glass. She didn't ever

drink more than a couple of glasses, and the last thing she needed was to make a fool of herself.

"Come in!" she called, hoping Ryan would hear her.

Hercules went bounding down the hall and a second later the door clicked.

Jess took a deep breath, ran her hands down her jeans, then stepped out to greet him. This was ridiculous. She'd seen Ryan a handful of times now. First-time nerves were one thing, but there was nothing to panic about tonight.

"Hi, Ryan."

He was crouched down giving Herc a scratch. When he looked up she temporarily lost the ability to move. His eyes locked on hers, bright blue, serious yet laughing, drawing her in as if she'd never be let back out again.

"Hi." He stood and they both watched as Hercules took off down the hall again. "You look great."

Jess looked down and felt awkward. She was only wearing jeans, an embellished T-shirt that dressed her outfit up and a pair of heels. Her cheeks were flushed, she could feel the heat in them—and her hands could have been shaking. She was so off balance she wasn't even sure.

She went to turn down the hall, but he stopped her with a hand to her wrist.

"Hey."

When she turned Ryan took a step forward and pressed a kiss to her cheek before putting space between them again.

"You act like no one ever gave you a compliment before."

His voice was low, almost a whisper, and it made a shiver lick its way down her spine. She swallowed, hard.

"I'm not."

The last compliments she'd had had been from a man who told her what he thought she wanted to hear, but there'd never been any substance to his words. The reason she was embarrassed now was because from the look on his face, Ryan meant what he said.

"I don't say what I don't mean," he assured her.

She didn't doubt that. "I know, it's just…"

"Jess?"

She felt uncomfortable being scrutinized.

"I find you not receiving compliments by the bucket-load hard to swallow," he said. Ryan tucked his fingers beneath her chin and smiled down at her, his eyes locked on hers, body so close. "You look beautiful tonight and you need to believe it."

Jessica fought against the urge to pull away from him. Instead of giving in to her instincts she made herself smile, forced herself to behave like the grown-up woman she was. "Thanks," she whispered.

He grinned and let his fingers fall from her skin. "Much better."

She turned before he had the chance to do anything else. She was nervous, scared.

Exhilarated.

So much for telling herself this was going to be a casual dinner with a friend, that there was no need to panic. She doubted there was much *friend* left in the equation between her and Ryan anymore. Part of her had hoped he would want more, and the other part told her that friend was as good as it got. Even after their kisses.

Now she wasn't so sure she was ready for the something more.

Ryan was a hot-blooded male who had suddenly, just from looking at her, from touching her, made his intent very clear.

The way her body was reacting told her she felt the same, no matter how much she wanted to deny it.

Maybe that glass of wine hadn't been such a bad idea after all.

Jessica didn't taste a mouthful of her food. She opened her mouth, forked spaghetti in delicate twirls and forced herself to swallow. But the only sense she had was of the man sitting across from her.

She'd forgotten everything else. Had no control over her other senses. Or maybe she did and they were too overloaded on Ryan. She was drunk on the sight of him, the feel of him, the look of him.

The taste of him.

She remembered only too well what his lips felt like on hers, how her body had felt when she was tucked against him, wrapped in his embrace. And after the way he'd touched her in the hall before, the way he felt had been the only thing she'd thought about since.

"This is great."

At least Ryan seemed to be enjoying the food.

Jessica took another sip of wine. She was going to tell him not to be silly but she remembered only too well what he'd said earlier about taking a compliment.

"Thanks."

She wished she could say more, could come up with something more savvy and chic, but her brain just wasn't cooperating. Her tongue was swollen like it was bee-stung, not letting her communicate properly.

It was stupid. She was a confident, capable woman and there was no excuse. She had to get a grip. Jessica cleared her throat and set down her fork. "So tell me about George. You two looked like you were having a good time yesterday?"

Ryan's entire face seemed to light up.

"We had a fantastic time. It's like we've really connected."

She smiled. It was good to hear.

"But I have to thank you, you know."

Jess gulped. Her? "Why me?"

Ryan put his own fork down and reached for her hand across the table. "Because you gave me the confidence to make it happen. I don't think I could have done it without you."

Jessica forced herself to look up and meet his gaze. His hand over hers was doing something to her, making her body feel hot all over, every inch of it.

"I don't think I did anything, Ryan. I was just honest with you."

He squeezed her hand, his eyes never leaving hers. She could gaze into them all night, lose herself in the ocean-blue depths of them, become mesmerized. She wondered if anything had ever looked so beautiful before. The way he was looking at her, the softness she saw there.

The honesty.

All this time, she'd thought it would be impossible to ever truly trust a man again. Told herself it couldn't happen.

But the way Ryan was watching her, the genuine feeling he conveyed through his gaze, the way the skin around his eyes crinkled ever so lightly in the corners when he watched her, his smile upturned to match his expression: all of these things told her that trust and honesty *was* possible with a man.

She'd just chosen the wrong one before. And let herself believe that he represented the entire male population.

"I went to him, Jess. I went to him because you told me to, because you told me I had to confront the past and be honest with him."

She looked down, unable to match his stare any longer. "I told you what anyone else would have."

Ryan shook his head. "That's the problem." He dropped the contact with her hand and raised it to her cheek instead, his fingers resting against her skin.

Jess pushed in, lightly, toward his touch. Fought the urge to close her eyes and sigh into his caress.

"I've never told anyone else what I told you in my letters. You're the first person I've been honest with in a long while."

She glanced up at him again, her breath catching in silent hiccups in her throat.

"It started because I trusted you on paper, and now I know I can trust you in real life, too."

She didn't know what to say. But when Ryan kept the contact with her face and raised his body, leaning over the table toward her, she knew exactly what to do.

Jessica raised her face to meet his, parted her mouth for his kiss. For the brush of his lips that she knew were coming.

Ryan took her mouth, gently at first and then with a hunger that scared her. She was barely conscious of him standing, of the way he had moved closer, until he pulled away and left her lips tender and alone.

She stifled the moan that fought to be heard deep within her throat.

But Ryan didn't leave her alone for long. He stalked around the table like a big game animal on the hunt. His large frame towered above her, then he dropped to his knees in front of her. She parted her own knees slightly so he could move closer to her. He was so tall that even with her sitting on the chair he wasn't much lower than her.

Jess just watched him—the rise and fall of his chest, and the way his eyes fell to her lips. She tried not to think about the what-ifs. Fought against the voice in her head that told her to take things slow, to stop now before it went too far.

Because Jessica knew they had already crossed that line. They'd already gone too far and she was powerless to do anything about it.

"Ryan."

He circled his arms around her waist, making her feel safe. Wanted. She slowly raised her hands and let them flutter to his shoulders, not sure where to touch him, and then they found his hair. Jess ran her fingers through the soft strands then stopped, fingertips on the back of his head as she bravely urged him forward.

He waited for her. Hardly let out a breath as he watched her and waited. Like he was leaving it up to her, wanted her to tell him it was okay.

And she didn't disappoint him, was powerless to do anything but make the next move. Jessica kissed him like she'd never kissed a man before. Kept her hands on him, drawing him to her, pressing herself closer to him as their lips danced, his arms still wrapped around her.

She only dropped her hold when she knew he wasn't going to pull away, to run her hands down his arms, drawing in a sharp inhale as she found bare skin.

His lips became more insistent on hers. Teasing her. Showing her how much he wanted her. And oh, did she want him, too. More than she'd ever wanted to be close to a man before.

"Ryan," she said his name again. "Are you sure…"

He just kissed her more deeply, ignoring her words. She took his lack of reply as a yes.

Jessica let her fingers keep exploring, reached the hem of his T-shirt and pushed it up, letting one hand discover the contours of his hard stomach, muscles firm against her touch.

His belly quivered, but he didn't move. Only moaned against her mouth.

She took it as encouragement.

Jess tugged, breaking their kiss to pull his T-shirt over his head, and Ryan didn't resist.

He shrugged out of it in a second and had his arms back around her before she could properly drink in the sight of him.

But she pushed him back, lightly.

"You have a tattoo," she whispered.

Wow.

"Yeah." He shrugged.

If the sun-kissed golden skin and hard muscles weren't enough, hadn't already taken her breath away, the tattoo came as even more of a shock.

She'd never dated a guy with a tattoo before. Had always thought they were for bad boys, and she'd never gone for that type. But on Ryan? It looked incredible.

"You're staring." His voice was low, husky.

Jess gave him a sideways look and smiled. Shyly. "Does it mean anything special?"

The black ink carved out a beautiful eagle, wings open, covering his entire shoulder and down his upper biceps. She'd never liked the idea of a tattoo, but this was something else. Made him look even stronger, tougher. Exciting.

His response was another shrug. She hoped she hadn't made him self-conscious about it.

"It's a special forces thing. I got it after my initiation with all the other snipers."

She leaned forward, bent to touch her lips to his shoulder, kissing down every inch of the inky black image. She let her fingers trail over the small, dark pink scar that showed where his keyhole surgery had been.

Ryan moaned and tightened his hold on her. It made her smile, pleased that he liked it, that he wanted her touch.

"Jess."

The way he said her name made it sound like a warning. He tugged at her hair, gently, to pull her had back up. She ignored him, slowly running her lips up his neck, making him wait before she returned to his mouth.

She stopped, hovered her lips beside his before kissing him.

Ryan didn't hold back at all this time. He took her face in his hands, kissed her again, and then stood, lip still tangled, arms around her body.

He only had to look at her to ask her the question. To tell her what he wanted.

The way he watched her, touched her, caressed her, told her everything she needed to know. Left only one question between them.

"Yes," she whispered, tugging his hand.

He dropped a feather-light kiss to her lips. "Are you sure?"

She tucked in tight against him, nuzzled her mouth

to the tender spot between his shoulder and neck, before taking his hand and leading him to the stairs.

No, she wasn't sure. Showing her body to a man again had been something she'd feared since her operation. All she knew was that she wanted to be with this man, right now, more than anything else in the world.

And that meant swallowing her fears and taking a big step forward. Maybe he wouldn't notice the difference? she found herself wishing…

Ryan felt as if his whole body was on fire. He wanted this woman like he'd never wanted a woman ever before.

And he was too weak to do what he most wanted. To scoop her up into his arms and carry her to her bed, to make her feel light and wanted in his embrace. He hated not having the strength in his arm, but then if he hadn't been injured he wouldn't be here right now. And he knew where he'd rather be, given the choice.

But even though he couldn't lift her like he wanted to, he could enjoy the weight of her hand in his and the promise in her eyes as she sent a shy glance back over her shoulder at him.

He'd never been nervous before, not with a woman, not like this. But it had been a long time since… He tightened his jaw and pushed the thoughts away. Now was not the time to think about the past.

The problem with Jessica was that she wasn't just another girl. A one-night stand. He hadn't been with a woman he felt this serious about since his wife.

She was rather like his wife—not physically, but the same type of woman. He didn't want to hurt her in any way, do anything that might compromise what they had. Because she meant too much to him. But right now he was powerless to stop what was about to happen, and it was too late to start thinking about why this was a bad idea. He was the one who'd started it, and he certainly wasn't going to not follow through.

Jessica stopped at what he presumed was her bedroom and dropped his hand. She touched the door frame, looked over her shoulder and gave him an even shyer smile than before.

"You joining me?"

Ryan gave Jessica a brave grin back. "Yes."

It seemed to settle her, looked like relief crossed her eyes, softening her face.

He was going to ask her again whether she was sure, whether this was what she really wanted, but then she disappeared into the room. Ryan hesitated for a moment before following her in.

Jessica was standing, waiting for him, like she didn't know what to do. He hated seeing her look unsure, uncertain and nervous, but he knew what he could do to make her feel better. To make sure she knew how much he wanted her.

Ryan tried not to but he knew he stalked her across the room. He wrapped both arms around her, sweeping her to him, before walking her backward until her legs touched the base of the bed.

"Ryan…" His name caught in her throat, and it made him smile.

"Yes?" He arched an eyebrow before taking up on her neck again, where he'd last kissed her, letting his lips tease her skin.

She didn't say another word.

He already had his shirt off but Jessica was fully clothed. He tipped her back and gently let her fall, before moving to cover her, to lie half above her.

She blinked and kept her eyes downcast, but he tipped

her chin up and kissed her lightly on the nose then on her lips. At the same time he touched his other hand to her T-shirt, curling his fingers around it and raising it, pausing to give her the chance to say no.

Jessica responded by wriggling to rid herself of the top.

His gaze fell from her face to her skin, eyes dancing over her lacy red bra, the way her breasts filled it to almost overflowing.

"The light," she whispered.

Ryan shook his head. "No."

He stopped when he saw the panicked look on her face.

"Please." Her voice held urgency, desperation.

"Okay," he said as got up again, crossed the room and flicked off the switch. "Your call."

It didn't matter how much he wanted to watch her, to drink in the sight of her, he would do as she asked. He wasn't doing anything to compromise what was happening between them.

He stopped, in the dark, letting his eyes adjust.

Before using all of his willpower not to rush across the room and pin her down to devour her, piece by piece.

Jessica felt like she was blushing all the way down to her toes.

She wanted to stop him, to tell Ryan she couldn't go through with it, but if she told him that she'd be lying to herself.

She wanted him.

She just didn't want to know his reaction when he realized her breasts weren't natural.

It was the first time she'd been intimate with a man

since her reconstruction, since she'd gone through her treatment, and it scared her. She hadn't wanted him to see them bare, didn't want to see his reaction, either, but as soon as he touched them he'd surely know. They weren't soft and natural as they'd once been. Now there was the undisguisable firmness of silicone, and she was embarrassed about it.

Ryan's hand skimmed her arm then trailed slowly down the edge of her breast.

She took in a deep breath. This was it. The moment she'd dreaded for almost a year.

"You're beautiful."

Jessica closed her eyes and tried not to cry, fighting happiness and tears at the same time. As confused as she'd ever been.

She tried not to shake her head. Thank goodness the light was off so she didn't have to see the look on his face when he realized.

"You are. You're more beautiful than I ever could have imagined you'd be."

Jessica wanted to tell him she wasn't, admit what he'd find when he took off her final layer, but she held her words in, too scared to say them out loud.

Ryan stopped, as if he were questioning her, but Jess responded by staying still, waiting for him.

She held her breath. Terrified.

When his hand touched her bra, her entire body went stiff, rigid.

She couldn't do it.

"Stop."

His hand hovered then fell.

"I can't, Ryan," she whispered, distraught.

He dropped his hands to hers, and lowered himself to rest beside her. "Tell me what's wrong."

Jessica closed her eyes and pushed away the pain. Tried to figure out what exactly she could tell him.

"I have, well…"

He brushed the back of one hand gently across the side of her face, touching her cheek with the softness of a feather.

"We don't have to do anything you don't want to do."

Jessica smiled bravely at him. She did want to, that was the problem, but she didn't know how to deal with the embarrassment of what he was about to find.

Because even with the lights out, without being able to see, he would be able to feel. The scars were minor, the surgeon had done a great job, but the evidence was real and he would notice. There was no way not to.

She took a deep breath.

"Ryan, I have scars. I don't want…"

"Shhhh." He bent forward and kissed her, lips hovering over hers. "You don't have to explain anything to me."

She shook her head. "I do. My breasts, they're…"

He waited, fingers stroking her hair.

"I have scars because I had surgery. My breasts aren't real," she finally blurted out.

Ryan didn't say anything. He dropped another kiss to her lips before trailing his way down her neck, delicately across her collarbone, until he reached the lacy edge of her bra.

He paused and looked up at her. She could make out his face even in the dark.

"You're beautiful, Jessica, and I don't care what you've had done or about any scars."

With an incredible sense of relief exploding inside her, her body felt like it had turned into a marshmallow.

Her fears faded, and her body responded to his touch again. By his lack of reaction, he obviously just thought she'd had a breast augmentation. Realizing she'd managed to put off telling him the truth for a little longer, she trembled. Right now, he didn't need to know why she'd had cosmetic surgery. If he didn't care, then why should she?

Her body still thrummed with tension as he slipped off her underwear, but she forced herself to enjoy his touch. She couldn't help but stiffen when he kissed first one breast then the other, his fingers gliding softly over her skin.

"See, they're beautiful, just like I knew they'd be," he whispered. "Just like the rest of you."

Jessica finally relaxed into his touch, closed her eyes and sighed as his hands explored her body.

Tonight was about feeling good and enjoying herself. Losing herself in the moment. All this time she'd been terrified of showing someone her new body shape, worried what the reaction would be and if she'd even want to be intimate again.

But this—this was what she'd needed. To feel loved and wanted by a man like Ryan. A man who made her feel like she was the most beautiful woman in the world, like he truly wanted her.

Even if it was only just for tonight. Or until he went away again. Because if the light had been on, she could have looked into his eyes and seen his honesty, his integrity. Yet what she couldn't see in his eyes, she could feel in his touch.

When Ryan inched his way back up her body and started to kiss her again, she pushed away her barriers, made herself think of nothing but the way he was touching her. The way his fingers felt against her skin, and the way his lips brushed hers in a motion she'd never tire of.

If this wasn't heaven, then she didn't know what was.

CHAPTER EIGHT

Dear Jessica,
It's funny, now I know I'm coming home for sure
and that we're going to meet. I should have asked
you for a photo, but then we probably don't look
like either of us expects.

You know, I've enjoyed this life for so long, but
now the thought of coming back and sleeping in
a comfortable bed, of not having to get up at the
crack of dawn, sounds pretty appealing. I can
hardly imagine what it will be like not to be with
my unit, here in the desert, because it's been so
long. But I'm sure looking forward to meeting
you.

I'll see you soon.
Ryan

RYAN WOKE WITH a smile on his face. It had been a long
while since he'd woken up grinning, but then it had also
been a long time since his arm had been taken captive
by a beautiful woman.

Jessica lay in the crook of his arm, face turned into
him, cheek against the edge of his chest. Her mouth was
slightly parted, her long hair falling over his skin and
spilling out onto the white pillow.

He didn't move, hardly let himself even breathe. Ryan could have stayed there forever, watching her. Content in what had happened between them. In the way his trip home had turned out after so many months of dreading it, after years of denying himself the luxury of returning. Of putting up barriers and refusing to confront what he'd left.

When he'd promised his son that this tour of duty would be his last, it had been a decision he'd made as a father.

But now? Deep down, he knew that part of that decision had been influenced by how he felt about Jessica. He wanted to come back for his son, but he also wanted more from this woman lying in his arms. Part of his decision had been because he wanted a real chance at making a future with her, too.

And that meant he had to let her in. A week ago, he'd have never thought it possible, but now he wanted to open up to her. To tell her the final chapter he'd kept behind lock and key from everyone but himself until now.

Jessica stirred. He shifted his body to face her, looking at her face as she started to wake.

Her eyes opened slowly, fluttered, then her head dropped slightly as she realized he was watching her.

"Hey, you," he whispered, stroking his thumb across her cheek.

She smiled, but he could tell she was shy. "Hey."

Her voice was so low he only just heard her.

"What do you say I rustle up something for breakfast?" he offered.

She tucked her head down and snuggled against him, hair tickling his chest as she buried into his body and pulled the comforter farther over them in the process.

Jess planted a kiss to his collarbone and sighed into his skin.

He lay with her in his arms for a few minutes then dropped a kiss to the top of her head and wriggled back.

His stomach growled. Loud.

"As much as I want to stay like this, I think my body needs some fuel."

Jess laughed and rolled over.

"What's so funny?"

He propped himself up and looked down at her. She was still trying to hide from him, face partially covered, but she didn't look nervous any longer.

"Jess?"

She groaned then turned back toward him. "I probably shouldn't tell you, in case you change your mind."

He raised an eyebrow and watched her.

She groaned again. "You're the first guy to offer me breakfast in bed, okay?" She let her eyes meet his. "Here I was worried you'd make an excuse and bolt, and instead you offer to feed me."

Ryan leaned forward to kiss her, brushing the hair from her face so he could see her better. He liked that her trademark pink blush was starting to cover her cheeks again.

"I don't recall saying anything about breakfast in *bed* exactly, but it can be arranged. Although if I remember correctly, you never actually gave me dessert last night."

She responded by pushing him away and throwing a pillow at him. He caught it and grinned.

"Okay, okay! Your wish is my command."

He stood up and walked across the room. Most of his clothes were in a heap near the foot of the bed, but it was her silk robe hanging on the back of the door that caught his eye.

"Mind if I borrow this?" He plucked it from the hanger and held it up.

Jessica was blushing all over again but she nodded, sitting up with the sheet clutched to her chest.

He grinned and put it on, just managing to secure the pink satin with the flimsy tie. It barely covered him but it made her smile, laugh even, and right now he'd do anything to see those lips of hers upturned, those chocolate-brown eyes sparkling.

Even if he did have to make a fool of himself.

He was about to turn around and make a joke when he heard a phone ringing.

"Yours?"

She shook her head. "Nope. Your cell?"

It *was* his. He took off down the stairs and looked around for where he'd left it. Nowhere. He scanned the room and found it just as it stopped ringing.

When he flipped it open he saw he'd missed a few calls. All from the same number.

Ryan gulped.

His parents. Or his son. He hoped everything was okay. After so long being used to only thinking about himself, he should have at least phoned to tell them he wasn't going to make it home last night. Not that his parents would be worried, but George might be. He was going to have to change his habits if he was going to gain George's trust again.

He hit redial.

"Hello."

His son picked up almost immediately.

"Hey, George, it's your dad."

There was silence for a moment, before his son cleared his throat.

"I thought something had happened to you."

Ryan felt as though someone had reached into his chest and stuck a knife through his heart. If he was going to get this dad business sorted, he was going to have to start acting like a father, not a bachelor with no responsibilities.

"I, ah, ended up staying at a friend's place. I should have phoned."

There was silence on the other end.

"George?"

"Are you coming home soon?"

Ryan looked down at the pink robe, at his hairy legs poking out, and then turned to look at the stairs. He wanted to see his son, to be there for him, but he also didn't want to hurt Jess, and if he left now she'd think he'd used her. That he was as bad as the last guy who'd clearly broken her heart by not caring enough.

She deserved better than that. But then so did his son.

"I'm going to be a bit longer." He paused, cringing at the silence down the line. "But I'll be home soon, then we should grab some lunch, okay?"

"Yeah."

Ryan hated the way he felt when George hung up. Like he was being torn in two different directions. Yanked one way in his heart, then the other.

He sighed and put down the phone. Fifteen minutes ago he'd been on cloud nine, had felt like everything was going to work out perfectly, and now he was all messed up in his head again. He needed to do something to make things right, and that might mean talking to his boy about Jessica. Somehow.

"Is everything okay?"

Ryan turned to find Jessica standing nearby. He was pleased he'd put down the phone because it would have dropped from his hand and hit the floor.

She was wearing his T-shirt and what looked like nothing else. It only covered her down to the top of her thighs, and she had her ankles crossed, legs together, hair all mussed up and falling around her face. She must have found it while he was on the phone, which meant he'd missed seeing her walk into the room naked.

"Ryan?"

He realized he was standing there like an idiot, mouth hanging open. Her face was like an open question mark, eyes showing her confusion. He didn't like it. He liked what he saw, her big brown eyes watching him, so much skin on show apart from what was hidden beneath his shirt, but he hated that she was unsure of him.

Ryan crossed the room and wrapped his arms around her, smiling as he realized that she now smelled like his cologne. He kissed her neck, then her cheek, then her lips, hands buried in her hair.

"Everything is fine."

She pressed her face against his chest, fingers teasing his bare skin where her dressing gown didn't stretch enough to cover him.

"So where's breakfast then?"

He growled and slapped her bottom. Jess shrieked and jumped away from him.

"Any more naughty business and I'll take a photo of you like that," she threatened.

He followed her across the room, teasing her. "Oh, really?"

She giggled, darting away, one hand holding down his T-shirt. He couldn't help but smile at her modesty.

After the night they'd just had, here she was still innocent enough not to want him to see her bare in the daylight.

When she moved again he pounced, grabbing her wrists and pinning her against the wall.

"You win." She wriggled but didn't put up much of a fight.

Ryan held her, restrained her, taking the chance to kiss her before backing away.

"If I win, that means I get a prize."

He let go of her wrists and walked into the kitchen, taking a look in the pantry. Jess followed him, but she stopped to fill the jug.

"Coffee? That can be your reward."

He shook his head, reaching for a loaf of bread and the maple syrup.

"French toast?" he asked.

Jessica nodded.

"And my prize is that you say yes to lunch with me today."

She leaned back against the counter, eyes slanted slightly like she didn't believe him. "What's the catch?"

"My son's joining us."

Jessica gulped and watched Ryan's face. He wasn't kidding.

"Are you sure that's a good idea?"

He looked around. "Eggs?"

She went to the fridge and pulled out a tray, still waiting for him to respond.

Ryan nodded, but she could tell he was teetering on being unsure about it.

"I don't know if it's a good idea or not, to be honest.

But I'm not here long and I don't want to feel torn between the two of you. I want to enjoy you both and that
means not keeping us a secret."

Us. She took a silent, deep breath.

She had no idea what that even meant. What they
even were to one another. Last night had only further
complicated her jumbled thoughts.

This was supposed to be fun, something casual, but it
was starting to feel a whole lot more serious than that.

"When you say *us*..."

Ryan looked up as he cracked eggs into a dish.

"Jess, you mean a lot to me." He paused, before opening a drawer and reaching in and rummaging, emerging
with the whisk. "I want George to know how much you
helped me when I was away, and I don't know why I
should have to keep that a secret. If I'm going to make
things right with him, I need to be honest. About everything. And I think it might help to open up to him."

Okay. That sounded better. More like introducing
her as a good friend.

"So when I meet him you'll tell him we're..."

He smiled. "Close friends."

Right. "I just don't want you to push it with him. If he
thinks I'm your girlfriend it might make things difficult
for you."

Ryan dipped the first slice of bread into the bowl and
gave her one of his double-wattage grins.

"I'm not going to make this difficult for him. But I
have to be honest about what's going on in my life if I
want him to let me back in. Trust me again. I'll talk to
him beforehand, explain myself so he understands." He
paused. "I'm doing this for him. If I thought it wouldn't
be the right thing for him, I wouldn't even suggest it."

Jessica sighed. She knew what he meant, she just

wasn't convinced, personally, that his son was ready to meet her.

"Do you have any fruit?"

Jessica moved back to the fridge again. He seemed set on them meeting, and she wasn't going to hurt his feelings by saying no to the lunch. But she hadn't missed the look on George's face the other day, and something told her it might not be the right thing to do. Even if Ryan was doing his best to evade her questions right now, they had to tread carefully.

But he sure was good at changing the subject. "Go back up to bed," Ryan told her, pausing and leaning toward her to plant a kiss on her forehead. "I'll bring breakfast up when it's ready."

Ryan watched as Jessica's fingers played across his chest as they lay side by side. Breakfast had been started and then somehow quickly forgotten about, but he wasn't complaining.

He sighed as she snuggled in closer to him.

"What?"

Ryan propped himself up on one elbow, looking down at her. She was so beautiful it took his breath away. So innocent and giving, so kind.

He wasn't sure if this was the right time to bring this up, but he needed to tell her. Needed to be real with her, be honest if they were going to have a chance at that future he was starting to think about.

"I'm scared, Jess."

She tucked even closer into him and kissed his jaw. "Why? What do you have to be scared of?"

He tried not to frown. He had everything to be scared of. That was the problem.

"Because part of me wonders if I can do this being a

normal person thing. I don't know if I can forget what I've seen, and forget what I've thought and just be a human being again."

"You've always been a human being, Ryan. You've just seen things that most of us would be too scared to confront," she said.

"Sometimes I wonder if being in the army, serving overseas, takes the humanity from you and makes you into some sort of machine. It stops you from feeling, it makes it okay to just treat each day as a new opportunity. But in real life, you need to look back, too. You need to remember."

"See this?" Jessica let her fingers dance along his cheek to wipe at a tear. "This makes you human."

He smiled, just, from the corner of his mouth on one side.

She kissed his lips, softly, so he could only just feel it. He leaned forward as she pulled away.

"That makes you human, too." She rolled over and reached inside her bedside table and pulled out a letter. "See this?"

He would recognize it anywhere. One of the letters he'd sent her. "You kept them?"

"Every one. My drawer is full of them."

He reached for it but she pulled it away and tucked it back again.

"I don't even know which letter that was, or why it was on the top of the pile, but those letters? Each one told me you were a man who knew how to love and how to lose. That you were a man who could help save our country, who could help his men, and now here you are at home trying to be a man and a dad and a civilian."

"And?"

"And now I know that you can do it."

"Why?"

She pressed her face into his chest. He had no idea why she had so much faith in him, but it gave him a strength he'd worried he didn't have.

"Because now you're helping me and it's working," she told him, her voice muffled by his skin.

He smiled and puller her closer. "You do know that whatever I'm not sure about, whatever I'm worried about, doesn't mean I'm not absolutely sure about what's happening between us, right?"

Jessica sighed as she lay in his arms.

Ryan nudged at her breast with his finger, circling over her skin and tracing back up to her face. It was as if he couldn't stop touching her, and she felt the same about him.

One day he'd ask her about her scars, what had led to her cosmetic surgery, but he didn't care. Plenty of women enhanced their breasts, and she had obviously had her reasons.

"You're my second chance, Jessica."

She pulled up so her head was resting on her hand, propped by the pillow. "I wasn't aware you needed a second chance."

He needed to tell her now. Take that step to let her in completely. "You're my chance to make things right."

"It wasn't your fault your wife died, Ryan."

He smiled, sadly. He hoped she'd understand. "No, but I didn't love her like she deserved to be loved. She was my best friend in school, and I loved her like only a best friend can."

He didn't say what he really wanted to. Tell her how he felt right now. Because it seemed too soon, too fast.

Now he knew what true love really felt like.

"Did she feel the same way?"

Ryan shook his head and played with her hair, his arm resting on her shoulder. This was the part he hated to admit, even to himself. Why he felt guilt like a crawling parasite over his skin sometimes. He'd always wondered if maybe he hadn't loved her enough to save her.

"She loved me deeply, I'd always known it. I could see it in her eyes every time she looked at me, even when she was in hospital with machines bleeping every time she so much as blinked."

He stopped and she just watched him. Ryan wished he could tell what she was thinking. "I never lied when I told her I loved her. We got married when we were eighteen, she was already pregnant with George, and we were happy. We never argued, and I told her every day that she meant the world to me. And she did."

"But?"

He leaned forward and kissed the tip of her nose. He wanted to ask Jessica if it made him a bad person for thinking he was so pleased to have met her. That finding her meant he could finally forgive Julia for leaving him. But he didn't. Because part of him wasn't ready to admit that out aloud yet. And he had a feeling that maybe Jessica wasn't ready to hear it.

But what he was sure about was how he felt about her. The last twenty-four hours had proven to him how special she was. "There's no but. I just want to say thank you, Jess. For everything."

She smiled as a tear escaped from the edge of her own eye. He kissed it away as she whispered back to him.

"You're welcome."

CHAPTER NINE

Dear Ryan,
I know by now that you probably torture yourself
by thinking over things you should have done, but
there's no point dwelling on the past. Especially
on things you had no power to control. Before you
come home, I think you need to forgive yourself,
and let yourself move on.

Focus on what you have to do, stay safe and
promise me that you'll write to your son more
often. Even if you don't have much to say, just
put pen to paper.

We write to one another so often now that
you don't have any excuses not to write to him.
Okay?
Jessica

JESSICA COULDN'T HELP the sigh that escaped her lips.
She'd thought waiting for Ryan to arrive last night had
been nerve-wracking. How wrong she'd been. Waiting
to meet his son was far worse. The only consolation was
that she wasn't meeting his parents, too.

She walked into the park, clutching Hercules's lead
and telling herself it was worth it. They'd had a great
time last night. Make that super. And if he needed her to

meet his son, to keep things open and honest, and help to repair his relationship with George, then she didn't have much choice other than to go along with it.

But she was already feeling messed up in her head about what had happened. Not the physical side, but the way he'd opened up to her. She was starting to think that maybe he wanted more from her than she'd expected from him. The way he'd talked to her, the things he'd told her...

She'd told herself this thing with Ryan was meant to be casual. He was leaving soon. She was not available to the idea of anything serious, and yet it felt like they had gone from friends to something very serious, very fast.

Jess pushed her hair behind her ears and tried to shut off the voice in her brain telling her to run. No matter what happened today, she had to remember it was worth it. Ryan had made her feel incredible last night. He had made her realize that she could be wanted and loved again. Just because he was going away did not mean it wasn't worth every moment. Because it was.

She'd been so scared of showing a man her body, of opening up again and putting her heart out there. But Ryan had helped her through something she had thought was impossible to recover from. Once she'd gotten over the initial shock of him seeing her breasts, she hadn't thought about it again all night. After months of worrying, he'd made her thoughts vanish in less than a heartbeat.

Just thinking about him like that put a smile back on her face. Until she spotted them. And her anxiety came back like a troop of butterflies playing in her stomach.

Ryan raised a hand to wave. They were walking along

by the pond. She could see his son smiling, then watched as his face fell when he saw her. She wanted to run. But it was too late to back out now.

Instead she sucked up her courage and bent to let Hercules off the lead. The least she could do was let the dog have fun, chase some ducks while she tried not to find a hole to crawl and hide in.

"Jess!" Ryan called out and she mustered up a big smile again. Forced it on her face.

She waved back and watched as Hercules bounded up to them, before taking off to do laps back and forth along the water's edge.

"Hi, guys."

Ryan walked toward her and kissed her on the cheek. She tried to enjoy it, to experience that magical breath-lessness she usually felt when his lips touched her. But instead all she saw was the flush of George's cheeks as he looked the other way.

"I was telling George what happened with your dog the last time we were here," Ryan said.

The boy nodded, face still stained a patchy red.

Jess shook herself out of the slump she was in. She was the adult here, the least she could do was make it as easy on George as she could.

"Little Herc means the world to me," she said, taking a step away from Ryan, needing the breathing space as his boy watched them. "I can't believe I was so caught up in getting to know your dad that I almost lost him."

"Why did you start writing to my dad?" The boy's face flushed a deep red just asking her.

"Well…" She paused and looked at Ryan. He nodded at her to continue. "I wanted to show that I cared about what our soldiers were doing for us, for our country. I heard about a pen-pal program that was being run with the army, and somehow I ended up writing to your father, out of all the soldiers serving overseas."

Ryan moved closer to his son, hand on his shoulder. "When I told you that Jess made a huge effort to write to me, I meant that she wrote to me all the time. Every week. She helped me to see why I needed to come back home."

George took a few steps back then turned to face the water again. "What did she tell you?"

Jessica didn't know what to say. She was uncomfortable being made to feel like she was somehow a surrogate mother for the day. It wasn't a role she wanted to fill. She wasn't ready to face that kind of commitment.

"She guided me through dealing with my problems, we talked about everything and it gave me the strength to face what I'd left behind," Ryan explained.

"Did you talk about Mom?" George asked.

Jessica wanted to back away but she couldn't. She just stood there, feeling like an intruder.

"Yeah, about you and your mom."

George turned away, like he didn't want to talk about it anymore. It hadn't gone down that badly, but it hadn't exactly been great, either.

"Lunch?" She made the suggestion as the air became stale between them all.

Ryan looked at her gratefully. "Yeah, good idea."

She sat beneath a nearby tree on the grass and Ryan did the same. George didn't move.

Jess didn't want to be here any more than she guessed the boy did. It felt like she was intruding on something she had no right to be a part of.

"I hope you like sushi."

She nodded. At least lunch was going to be good. "Show me what you've got."

Ryan gave her a relieved look, reaching out to squeeze her hand before calling to his son. "You joining us, George?"

He slowly turned toward them, his eyes telling his entire life story. They looked sad, haunted almost, and Jess fought the sudden tug deep inside her that made her want to hold him, to comfort this boy who was so confused.

He just shrugged, but she knew he probably wanted to cry. To yell at her and ask his dad why he had to meet her at all.

"Hey, George, why don't you go get Hercules for me?" she suggested.

There was a small light in his eyes as she gave him the Get Out of Jail Free card.

"Either throw sticks into the water for him, or just get hold of him and bring him back," she told him.

George went off straight away and Ryan reached for her knee, his hand closing over it. "Thanks for that."

She took a deep breath. "I don't know if meeting George today was the best idea."

Ryan grimaced. "I know, but I did have a big talk with him before we came. Explained why I wanted him to meet you." He paused. "Sometimes the hardest thing is the best thing to do, even if it doesn't feel like it at the time, right?"

"I think him having to deal with me when you guys are only just starting to sort things out is too much." But part of her felt dishonest—because maybe, just maybe, it was just too much for *her* and yet exactly the right thing for George.

Ryan shook his head, jaw suddenly clenched a bit tighter, making him look more determined. His hand hovered then came to rest on her cheek.

Jess sighed at his touch.

"You mean something to me, Jess, and I don't want to keep things from him."

She turned her face to kiss his palm, wishing things could be more simple between them. That he wasn't going away, and that she didn't have to keep huge secrets from him.

"Ryan, you're going away soon." Jessica paused. "There's no need to cause complications when they don't even need to exist."

Now it was Ryan shaking his head. "I should have told you that I'm not leaving for good, Jess. If I didn't think we had a chance, that this didn't mean something, I wouldn't have let things go this far between us."

She swallowed, hard.

"In fact, I've already decided that this will be my last tour."

Silence hung between them.

Oh, my.

Was he serious?

She hadn't seen this coming. He'd been so determined to continue on with his career in the army, had made that so clear to her in his letters, it was the only reason *she'd* let things go this far. He'd even told her as much that first day they'd met.

Ryan was being so honest with her, and here she was keeping guilty secrets from him. All this time she'd thought it was men she couldn't trust, yet right now she was the one lying by omission. Who wasn't being up front about what she wanted and what she had to give. And now he was telling her that maybe they had a chance at a future. The one thing she'd thought he didn't have to offer her.

"Ryan…"

She didn't know what to say.

"Do you really think I would have jeopardized our friendship by making love with you if I was going to walk away and never look back?" She saw a flash of anger, of disappointment in his eyes. "You've done so much for me, the last thing I want to do is hurt you."

And yet from the sound of it, she was going to be the one doing the hurting.

Did that mean he wanted more from her? That he thought this was going to develop into something she hadn't possibly thought it *could* turn into?

Tears stung, pricked at the back of her eyes, but she fought them. She was used to putting on a brave face, to keeping her emotions to herself.

She wasn't emotionally available for a relationship. And she'd lied to him. If she'd just told him about the cancer in the first place, things would never have gotten to this point. It was her fault and no one else's.

"I think what you need to do is focus on your son," she said instead.

Ryan's eyebrows knotted as he drew them together. "Without you I wouldn't even *have* a relationship with my son."

She disagreed. He would have found a way to reconnect with George even if she hadn't been there for him. She looked up as Hercules landed in her lap. She cleared her throat as George appeared.

"Hey, buddy." She swatted at her dog as he tried to kiss her.

Ryan stayed silent.

"Thanks, George, he can be a handful sometimes."

The boy smiled at her and sat down. Hercules went straight over to him and had him laughing within seconds.

Ryan looked back at her, confusion in his eyes. She gave him a tight smile back. There was a lot unsaid between them, and from the look on his face, she'd hurt the one man who had given her a glimpse of what she might one day have in the future. An honest, caring, kind man who deserved better than what she could give him right now.

When he found out what she'd kept from him, he'd be hurt beyond belief. So the only thing she could do was make sure he never, ever found out. Which meant she had to make a decision and stick to it. Maybe it was time to walk away. Either that or she had to brave up and give him the chance to accept her for who she really was. The very thought made her shiver with fear.

"Sushi, right?"

Ryan gave her a confused smile and took three trays out of the plastic bag he'd been carrying.

She smiled back, but inside she was crying a thousand tears. He'd opened up to her, and she'd let him, because as his friend she owed it to him to listen and be there for him. What she hadn't realized was that when he'd told her this morning that he hadn't loved his wife *enough,* that just maybe he'd been trying to tell her something else.

Except she wasn't ever going to put him through that kind of heartache ever again.

CHAPTER TEN

Dear Ryan,
Have you ever thought about coming home for
good? I know you love what you do, but I often
wonder how long a person can live away from
their family. From their normal life.

Don't you miss being home? Or are you so
focused on your task over there that you don't
even let yourself think about what you're missing
out on back here?

Whatever happens, even if we don't end up
meeting, I want you to know that I think about
you and your unit every day. And I pray for your
safe return home one day soon.
Jessica

AFTER TOYING WITH her phone for what felt like forever,
Jessica put the key back in her car's ignition and gripped
the steering wheel.

Things hadn't gone well this afternoon. Not well at
all.

Somehow the perfect morning, waking in the arms
of a man like none other she'd met before, had turned
into the most dismal afternoon on record.

And no amount of grocery shopping or busying herself at home had helped the way she was feeling.

She needed to deal with this properly.

Finally she'd met the kind of guy she'd always dreamed of. Enjoyed the company of a member of the opposite sex, had a night that she would remember forever and had a man open up to her and tell her that she meant something to him.

Yet she was the one who'd managed to blow things. She wasn't ready for a relationship, had never thought whatever it was she had with Ryan could even have the chance of turning into something serious. Not when she'd expected him to be away serving again for goodness only knew how long.

So she either had to hurt him by coming clean and telling him about her past, and break her own heart in the process, and convince him that she liked him back but that nothing could happen, or call things off right now.

But in all the hours that had passed since she'd left him this afternoon, she hadn't figured out what to do. She cringed and put her foot down on the accelerator a little harder.

The way she felt around him was…indescribable and made her *want* to tell him the truth about her past. Yet would calling things off now be easier on him than telling him the truth? It would certainly prevent her from ever hurting him again like he had been over his wife's death, if he wasn't around to see her in the event that she became sick again.

If she wasn't driving she'd have banged her head against the wheel. It was all such a mess. Even without the added complication of his son, it was too much, too soon. Yet here she was, looking for his house,

determined to do *something* to make the afternoon turn
out better than it had so far.

She owed it to both of them not to leave things like
this.

Jess scanned the numbers on mailboxes until she
saw 109. Phew. His car was in the driveway. And it appeared to be the only one in residence. He'd mentioned
that his parents were away for the night, had gone off to
visit friends. And his son was to be at a friend's place,
too, or so he'd said earlier.

That meant it was now or never.

Jessica stepped from the car and walked up the path.
It was a nice house, nothing flashy, but modern and
solid. A small family home. She guessed it had been
Ryan's when his wife was still alive. He'd told her that
he owned it, but his parents lived there and took care
of the place while he was gone.

Jess knocked on the door.

"Coming."

His voice hit her in the chest, pierced her in the
gut.

Suddenly the idea of calling things off was definitely
not an option. That left her with one possibility on her
list: she could leave it up to him, tell him the truth and
let him decide if he could face the possibility of the pain
of cancer again.

The door swung back.

"Jess?"

She stood there, awkward, handbag clutched under
her arm. Unsurprisingly, Ryan looked unsure. She'd
bolted from the park straight after lunch, so he was
probably wondering why she was even here.

"Can I come in?" she asked.

His face relaxed and he held out his hand. "Come here."

She softened at his touch, let him draw her in, hold her. Comfort her. Even though she didn't deserve it.

"I'm sorry about earlier," she mumbled against his chest.

Ryan kissed her forehead and stepped back. "My fault, not yours. It was too much, too soon, right?"

She nodded, eyes cloudy with tears. It felt so right to be tucked against him, to find comfort from his body, but she knew what she had done was wrong. For once she had to admit that her brother had been right. If she'd been honest from the start she wouldn't be in this position right now.

"George is out?"

Ryan took her hand and led her down the hall. "Yep, at his friend's house. He looked pleased to get out of here."

She relaxed. It was just the two of them. Time to finally clear the air and come clean.

She followed him into the living room, toying with her bag, before sitting down on the sofa. He sat down, too, falling beside her, knees knocking hers, thigh brushing against her own.

Jessica felt rotten. The look on his face was so open, so kind, and she was about to bring up something that she'd wanted so badly to keep hidden.

And in the process she was going to hurt him.

But when she looked at him, saw the honesty there, remembered the way he'd treated her last night, she owed him nothing less than the truth.

"Ryan, I need to talk to you about something."

"Sounds serious." He grinned and took her hand, fingers circling her palm.

Why did this have to be so hard?

"It's ah, about your wife. Sort of."

Ryan's hand fell away from hers. She wasn't sure if he was angry or just plain unsure.

"You told me that you couldn't go through that again. That what happened with your wife…"

His face had gone from soft to hard. Like steel, braced for impact. "Is this about what I said earlier? I'm sorry if I scared you off, I just wanted you to know how I felt, that I wouldn't be doing this, misleading you, if I didn't think we had something special between us."

Jessica sighed. She didn't even know if she was doing the right thing now. Had no idea how to continue. But she had to try. Maybe she hadn't completely ruined what chance they might have had at a future together. Maybe he would understand.

"You opened up to me this morning, Ryan, and I think I owe you an explanation. I need to tell you something."

Ryan was a soldier. His life was all about walking away from his own personal issues and fighting for a greater cause. And yet he'd been brave enough to talk to her, to tell her the truth.

There was only so long she could run and hide from what had happened.

"You can tell me anything, Jess." He smiled at her so genuinely she wanted to cry. "Whatever you need to say, you can."

Jessica gripped his hand harder. Her eyes locked on his.

"I know what it's like to keep things hidden inside. I…"

He held her hand back, tight. "You do?"

A noise startled them both.

Jessica turned at the same time as Ryan. And came face-to-face with his son.

"George?" Ryan said, startled.

George looked at them and walked through the room and into the kitchen.

Jessica felt her heart sink to her toes. From the way they were cuddled up close on the sofa George probably thought he'd walked in on something he shouldn't have.

"Jess, can we…"

She smiled. There was nothing else she could do. Except maybe fall in a heap and sob her heart out. "Where's your room? I'll go and give you two some privacy."

He pointed down the hall. "Third on the left."

She touched his arm and walked away. "Take all the time you need."

Jessica opened the door to Ryan's room and stepped in. She could hear the sound of his voice as he spoke, but it was muffled and she didn't want to hear anyway. Whatever he needed to say was between him and his son, and she had enough on her own mind than needing to stick her nose in where it wasn't welcome.

It was weird being in Ryan's own personal space, and there was something disturbing about being there for the first time on her own. It made her think about what she hadn't managed to tell him. What she'd come here to say.

What she didn't want to tell him but had to.

Ryan was like a huge grizzly bear with a heart of gold, a man who'd known heartache like she could only barely understand, despite what she'd been through. A man who could kill an enemy with his bare hands yet was prepared to admit that he'd been a bad father in the past, and be honest with her that he couldn't face losing another person he loved again.

A man she wanted to love so bad, but was too scared of being honest with. It had been so much easier writing letters, when she could imagine that one day they could meet, that maybe he'd like her.

But she'd never considered that he'd be the kind of man she could fall in love with.

And deep down she knew she had already.

The reality of what she was feeling was harder to deal with. The reality of Ryan was a man who could cocoon her in his arms and make her feel safe. Make her think he could protect her from anything, maybe even from cancer. A man whose smile could make her forget every worry she'd ever had in her mind.

A man she could imagine having a life with.

So why hadn't she just been honest with him from the start? Why hadn't she told him when he'd opened up to her about losing his wife that first night over dinner?

Jessica sat on Ryan's bed, waiting for him. It seemed silly to be hiding out in here while he tried to deal with his son, but he was the parent. He was doing his best and she wasn't exactly helping the father-son relationship any. In fact, if they were both honest about it, her being in his life was probably the only remaining wedge stuck between him and his son.

But for some reason they had a connection that meant he was prepared to cause himself further heartache, to allow something to develop between them. And that only made her feel worse.

She'd been dishonest. And she knew that whatever he told her, as honest as he'd been with her, he'd prob-ably still run away once she told him the truth. And if, by some miracle, he didn't run, at the very least he'd be angry…no, furious with her.

Jessica fought the urge to lay back and cry. Instead she sat up straight and looked around her. Pushed her thoughts away. His scent was in the room, the bed still crumpled from where he'd slept the night before, but it wasn't a personal room.

Jessica stood and walked to the dresser. She let her eyes wander over a photo of George and a very old wedding photo of a Ryan she didn't recognize. It felt like she was already intruding, looking over his things like this, but she didn't stop. At least it was taking her mind off the way she'd behaved.

She moved to his wardrobe and stood in front of the door, fingers itching to open it. She listened. Just faintly, she could still hear the echo of voices in the living room.

Jessica looked at the closet, considering it as if it was a living, breathing thing. She opened the door so fast she couldn't change her mind, then staggered back, stumbling over her own feet.

Oh, my.

Ryan's U.S. Army camouflage pants and shirt hung from a thick, sturdy hanger. It was as if it was a person, the way his clothes hung with such a presence. The way they managed to steal the breath from her lungs, just hanging there like that. The uniform looked back at her like it had a soul of its own.

It was a part of Ryan, as much a part of his life as anything. It was the uniform he had worn when he'd been on tour last, what he'd no doubt been wearing when he'd sat and written to her. Maybe he'd even been wearing it when he'd read the letters she'd sent him.

It was a Ryan from another life, not the man she knew here.

Jessica wriggled her fingers, flexing them, before touching the fabric. Her fingers skimmed the strong, rough cotton of the camouflage shirt, nails tracing the nametag. McAdams. His name played in front of her eyes.

She touched down the legs. Same fabric, same feel. His boots, black and shiny, stood forlorn beneath the hanging uniform.

Jessica stepped closer, inhaling as she moved. It was clean, but not freshly laundered. She pulled it closer, hoping he'd never wear it again, then wishing she could stop herself from thinking that.

Tears stung her eyes. It was like a lump of wood was jammed in her throat, making swallowing impossible.

Why had it taken seeing his uniform to truly make her realize? The problem wasn't that she didn't want to be with Ryan, didn't want a future with him.

What she was scared of was losing him.

She'd never wanted it to be just a fling. To start with, she'd convinced herself that a few weeks or months with him was all she wanted. But from the moment they'd met…no, from the moment she'd felt the power of his words, she'd let herself hope that what they had could develop into something special.

She'd just been too scared to admit it to herself.

Deep down she didn't want him to go back at all. To leave her for even a moment. She wanted him to stay here, safe, to look after her instead of her country.

To protect *her*.

Something crinkled. Jessica let go and watched as the uniform swung back into place, like it was trained to hang straight, with perfection, like the way a soldier stands to attention. She looked over her shoulder, making sure she was still alone, then reached forward. Her hand connected with the front pocket of his shirt, and she heard the rustle again.

Something made her open it. Made her curious. Something told her she had to see what was there.

She undid the button and reached inside. It was a letter. Someone else might not have realized straight away, but she knew. Just like she knew instinctively that it was a letter for her.

After months of writing one another, she knew his handwriting almost as well as she knew her own. Even the way he folded his letters was precise, although this one was rumpled, like he'd been carrying it a long time.

The only difference was that this one wasn't in an envelope that had her name scrawled across the front. But when she unfolded the sheet, it had her name at the top of it.

She closed her eyes, wishing she could walk away from it, put it back and not read it. He hadn't given it to her, it felt wrong to look at it like this, but she couldn't *not* read it.

Turning away would be like denying a bee its pollen.

It was okay. If he didn't want her to read it, he wouldn't have been carrying it in his pocket, right? He'd probably just forgotten to post it, then he'd arrived home and he'd probably already told her what was written inside.

Or maybe not.

Either way she had to know what it said.

CHAPTER ELEVEN

Dear Jessica,
I've been sitting here since before sunrise, and
now it's almost midday. There's only one thing
I want to tell you. One thing I've been wanting
to tell you, so I'm just going to come out and
say it.

I think I love you, Jessica. I know I've never
met you, I know it's impossible to say this when I
could pass you in the street at this exact moment
and not know you. But one day, when we do meet,
I know I'll look at you and still feel the same.

A stranger might say that when we meet it won't
be the same, but something tells me it will be. That
there's a reason we managed to find each other
even though we're on opposite sides of the world.
I want to come home, and I think the reason is
you.

I love you, Jessica.
Ryan

JESSICA CAREFULLY REFOLDED the letter. She couldn't
breathe. She couldn't blink. She could barely move.

She forced herself to put the letter back in his

breast pocket, fumbled with the button, then closed the closet door.

No.

He couldn't love her. He couldn't.

Now that he'd met her, did he still feel that way?

Could he truly feel that way about her now?

Love her?

But in her heart, she knew the answer to that. Just like she knew that, without a shadow of doubt, she loved him back with all her heart. She'd fallen in love with him about the time she'd been released from hospital. When she'd realized that his letters were what had helped her pull through. Had given her the strength to recover.

All this time she'd been denying it, telling herself she was okay with a casual fling, with him going away again when she'd been in love with him since before he'd even arrived home.

But he couldn't love her back. He couldn't. And she wasn't going to wait around to find out.

He'd made it clear he couldn't live through the pain of losing a wife again. And even if he accepted what had happened to her, what she'd hidden from him, it wasn't fair to put him in that position again when even she didn't know what was going to happen to her.

Jessica grabbed her sweater and tried not to run. She walked out of his room, moving as quietly as she could, and made for the back door. He'd be better off forgetting her. If he knew the truth he'd be devastated, and he deserved better. If she left now, before things went any further, he'd hurt less than finding out the truth later on. A slightly broken heart was better than him knowing she had cancer and having to deal with what might happen to her in the future. What could reoccur.

She should have ended things before they got this far.

Should never have considered telling him about what she'd battled. It would be better for both of them, her leaving.

So why was it so hard walking away?

Tears fell down her cheeks like oversize raindrops falling from the sky to touch her. Shudders ran back and forth along the planes of her skin. Her bottom lip quivered like it was an instrument being played. But she kept on walking, until she was outside, and she didn't stop until she got in the car.

It was over. It had to be.

She only wished she could have said goodbye to him first.

When she walked back into her house, even the smile and waggy tail that Hercules threw her way couldn't make her happy, not even for a heartbeat.

"Come here."

She hardly had to whisper for Hercules to come to her. It was like he knew the power of his fur, knew how much she'd come to need him, to crave the warmth of his little body and the way he cuddled into her when she held him.

Jessica scooped him up and pressed him tight to her chest, her face falling to kiss his little head.

She tried not to think about Ryan but no matter what she thought of, his eyes were in her mind and the words of his final letter to her were ringing in her ears.

"Who's been phoning us, huh?"

She smiled at her loyal companion through her tears, walking with him in her arms to hit the flashing light on the machine.

"Hey, sis, haven't heard from you in a while. Call

around for a drink tonight if you're free, or whenever. See you later."

Jess smiled and hit delete. Steven might be overprotective and overbearing sometimes, but he was a great brother. And she knew that no matter what happened, how right he might have been, that he'd never say *I told you so*.

There was one more message.

She leant back on the counter and snuggled Herc.

"Ah, Jessica…"

She jerked forward, almost losing Hercules in the process. She would know that voice anywhere. It was her doctor.

"I'd hoped to speak to you in person but I haven't been able to get hold of you. Your test results came back and we're going to need to do some follow-ups. Please don't worry, it might not mean anything but as you know we need to be overcautious."

Jessica hit delete immediately.

She gently placed Hercules down on the ground and let her shaky hand reach for the glass in the sink. She turned the faucet on and filled the glass, drinking a few mouthfuls, before turning the water back on to let the cool liquid run over her wrists.

This couldn't be happening.

She eyed the telephone and wished she didn't know the doctor's number by heart.

Jessica sat down at the table, pen in hand. It didn't matter how she felt about Ryan, but what she wanted to say, it was just so hard to get it out, to make the words form in her brain and force them out in the open. The only way she truly knew how to communicate with him was on paper.

The words ran like the credits of a movie over and over, around and around in her mind, a well of dialogue she couldn't deny. Writing to Ryan came so naturally, usually, but no other letter had ever been so hard to write.

The doctor was right, it might be nothing, but she still had to tell Ryan. She owed him more than a lie now. She hoped he wouldn't think that he had to be there for her, that he couldn't walk away, even if he really wanted to. That somehow her cancer was his problem, too, when it wasn't.

Because unlike her ex, Ryan would probably feel obliged to be there for her now, if something was wrong, and she didn't want to be a pity case.

She needed to tell him the truth, and there was only one way she knew how to.

Jessica started to write.

Dear Ryan,

I don't know how we got here, or what we did to deserve this, but there's something you need to know about me that I never told you. Something that will no doubt make you want to run and never see me again.

When I started writing to you, I was in the hospital. I should have told you, but then I never thought I'd actually ever meet you. I never thought you would have to be the one supporting me. You were the soldier, the man away at war, and helping you made me feel better. You were the only person in my life who didn't treat me like a bird with broken wings. I could be myself, talk to you, laugh, without any strings.

But something happened when you arrived

here, into my life. Suddenly you weren't just a soldier, a faceless person who needed a friend. You were a man and I was a woman. So I didn't tell you about my cancer.

Before you, cancer was all I thought about. Then I thought I'd beaten it. Maybe I still have, but I don't know for certain yet. Either way I owe you an explanation for why I ran out on you earlier today, and why I'm going to disappear from your life forever.

I need to go back and see my specialist, Ryan, and so I think it's best we don't see each other again. You have George to deal with, and my being with you was complicated enough even before I plucked up the courage to tell you about my past.

You mean so much to me, but I can't put you through this, not after what you've seen. What you've gone through in the past with your wife, and what you made so clear you could never cope with living through again. I should have come clean then, been honest with you, but I was scared you'd walk away, and I wasn't ready to lose you so soon after meeting you. I wanted to enjoy your company while you were here, enjoy our friendship, although I can see now that was selfish of me.

Please know that I love you, Ryan. If we'd met in another lifetime, maybe we could have had something amazing together. I'm sorry, for what it's worth, and I will never forget you so long as there is breath in my body.

Yours always,
Jessica

Jessica wiped at the tears falling in a steady stream down her cheeks, but one still managed to plop onto the paper. It didn't matter. In her heart she knew he'd probably shed his own tears when he found her note, and she deserved to feel bad over what she'd done to him.

What she'd kept from him.

She picked up the letter, folded it, then placed it in an envelope. Jessica scrawled his name across it and picked it up, her bag in the other hand.

Earlier he'd phoned, telling her he wasn't sure what had happened before but that he'd be around later tonight to see her. To make sure she was okay.

Jessica dialed her brother's number.

"You okay?"

She smiled into the earpiece. Her brother meant the world to her. "The specialist has agreed to see me in the morning."

"You want me to come with you?"

"No, I'll be fine." She hoped. "If it's okay with you I'm going to come over soon with Herc so he can hang out with you tomorrow while I'm gone."

"You want to stay here the night?"

She tried not to cry. "Yeah, if that doesn't mess up your evening."

"Get in the car, sis, I'll have dinner waiting."

She hung up and picked up her keys.

Hercules was at her heel and followed her outside. Jessica only paused to lock the door and tape the envelope to the timber, just below the handle. She was glad she wasn't going to be around to see the look on Ryan's face. Just walking away from what she'd written was like a stake was being forced through her heart.

* * *

Ryan held his son tight and gave him a pat on the back. Man-to-man kind of stuff.

George smiled when he released him.

He hated that Jessica had had to leave, that his heart-to-heart with George had taken so long, but he'd have time to explain himself to her tonight. What mattered was that he'd been honest with George about his feelings for Jess, and now he had to be honest with her about them, too.

"You sure you don't mind if I leave you here for a bit?"

George shook his head. "Nah, go see her."

"Because if you'd rather me stay here I will."

His son rolled his eyes. "I get it. Just go, all right?"

Ryan gave him another slap on the back and stood, feeling good about how things were turning out. Finally.

"Guess I need to stop running for good, right?"

George just watched him.

"It's time for me to put down my roots again here, son. You know I meant it the other night when I said this would be my last tour, didn't you?"

He received a nod in return. Ryan gave George one final look, to reassure himself he'd be okay, then pulled on his jacket and found his car keys.

He'd finally found out what it meant to be a father again, and he wanted to be there for George. Had spent the better part of the afternoon opening his heart up to him and making sure he understood what his priorities were. Made sure he knew that his bringing Jessica into their lives was because what he felt for her was real. And what she'd done for them, the way she'd helped him man up to his son, was why he was prepared to fight for his right to be in both of their lives.

If there was one thing this injury had taught him, it was that he wasn't invincible. Or immortal.

He was desperate to speak to Jessica now. Whatever she'd been upset about telling him couldn't change his mind, even if she was nervous about getting something off her chest.

Opening his soul to her had been less painful than he'd thought, and after having a long talk with George, he had no intention of mucking up a future with Jess. Not now that his son understood what she meant to him.

It was now or never.

Ryan pulled up outside Jessica's house and walked up the path. There were no lights on inside and the curtains weren't drawn.

Maybe she hadn't got his message? His stomach flipped, anxiously. He hoped nothing had happened to her.

Ryan decided to go and knock anyway. She could be taking a nap, reading in her room without the light on. He wasn't going to back down now, not when he'd mustered the courage to open up to her. To tell her what she needed to know about him, and to admit how he really felt about her.

As he neared the door, he saw something white moving ever so slightly in the breeze. He squinted. It was almost dark, but he could tell it was an envelope. He'd waited for enough of them over the last year to know the exact size of the stationery she used.

Ryan stopped a foot from the door and reached out to touch it. Jessica's soft, scrawly handwriting stood out and beckoned him, called to him as it always did.

He'd loved receiving her letters when he was away, had treasured every one, but this one felt different.

This time when he saw his name, it made him want to drop it. Why would she have left him a letter? She could have called or waited for him, or scribbled a note on the door telling him when she'd be back.

The formality of this one felt all wrong. His name on the outside. The envelope. The darkness of the house in contrast to the white of the paper.

Ryan pushed his thumb beneath the seal and slowly took the letter from it. He walked back to the car so he'd have enough light to read it. There was no point knocking on her door, she'd clearly left this for him, and she wouldn't have pinned it there if she'd been inside.

He opened his car door and dropped into the driver's seat, feet still firmly planted on the road. He flicked the interior light on and held the note up.

Ryan felt the kick of betrayal, of pain, the moment he read her words. They hit him like a heavy man's fist to his stomach.

Jessica had lied to him.

She'd lied to him and she didn't even have the guts to tell him to his face.

He finished her words, eyes first skimming then rereading more slowly what she'd written. What she'd written on paper rather than tell him to his face.

Ryan dropped the letter then bent to retrieve it, screwing it up into a tight ball and throwing it out onto the sidewalk, not even able to bear having it in the car with him.

He sat, he couldn't do anything else.

Why? Why hadn't she just told him? What had he done to make her think she had to hide herself from him? To think she had to deal with all his problems yet not share her own?

Ryan tried to calm himself down. Tried to put his training in place and stay collected, to keep his mind settled.

But he couldn't. Fury charged within him like a tornado that built itself up to rip homes from the ground and spit them out again all torn and broken. His face was burning hot, fists clenched at his sides.

No! He was *not* going to let her just walk away like this. He'd finally opened up, acted like the man he so wanted to believe he was, and she'd just disappeared.

Ryan swallowed, over and over, trying to fight something he hadn't felt in so long. Sadness. Gut-wrenching, heart-breaking sadness. Guilt and pain like he'd thought he'd never have to experience again.

Tears stung in his eyes but he was powerless to stop them. They wet his cheeks then streamed down his jaw. He wiped at them, furious, but he couldn't stop the way he felt, or the way his body was reacting.

He wasn't the kind of guy who cried, for heaven's sake!

Ryan pulled his arm back and made a fist, pummelling the steering wheel. His fingers and wrist exploded with pain upon impact, his upper arm and shoulder throbbing within seconds.

His physio was going to kill him, but he didn't care.

What he cared about right now, right at this moment, was the woman who'd run from him. Who'd thought he wasn't man enough to deal with her past, when she'd been so caring about his.

He hung his head, nursing his arm against his chest, and ordered himself to stop crying.

He couldn't lose her. Not now. If she didn't want him, if he didn't mean to her what she did to him, then fine. But he was not going to lose another person he loved, however long they might have together. He wasn't going to live with any regrets this time. *If* her cancer had returned, if she was that sick, then he was going to suck up his memories and his pain and deal with it. He was going to be there for her.

Now all he had to do was find her and tell her that.

Ryan got out of the car, slammed the door shut and wiped at his face. His hand and arm still hurt but he didn't care. He stood, fists clenched, trying to figure out what to do.

He didn't care if she'd had cancer. He didn't care how angry he was, or how much he wanted to shake her and tell her how stupid she'd been. He no longer even cared that she'd lied to him. He realized she had thought it was the right thing to do, just like he'd thought staying away from home so long was the right thing to do.

He would do anything for Jessica, and even if it meant facing his biggest fear, he would be there. This was his chance to prove himself to her once and for all.

He had two options. Find Bella. Or turn up at her brother's place.

Bella was the easier option, and probably the more logical one, but if confronting her brother was what he had to do, then he'd turn up on his doorstep and not leave until he had an answer. He didn't care what it took. What he had to do. Even if her brother gave him a black eye for upsetting her and making her run.

Ryan was going to find her and tell her how he felt.

Whatever the consequences.

CHAPTER TWELVE

Dear Ryan,
Everything is fine here. Nothing really to report.
Your letters are always so much more interesting
than mine! I'm just busy with my painting and
life in general, sorry I can't entertain you with
anything more exciting.

Not long now until you're home, right? You
must be so looking forward to stepping off that
plane.
Jessica

JESSICA KNEW WHY she was feeling guilty. She knew
why she had had to run, because she was scared of feeling like she had once before.

In love. With no power over her future.

Scared.

She couldn't deal with feeling like that, not now. Her
focus had to be on healing herself, on *protecting* herself. And that's why she'd had to spend the night at her
brother's place. She didn't have the strength to deal with
being back here at the hospital and facing Ryan, too.

It was like she was only half the woman she'd been.
The cancer had done that to her. Stripped away her
hopes and dreams for the future and made her question

her every move. It had taken away the part of her that made her feel like a woman. And she just didn't want to put another human being through what she'd seen her family go through.

Yes, Ryan had made her realize that her cosmetic concerns were unfounded, but the reality of him dealing with her past, with her *cancer,* meant she'd had no choice other than to leave him.

To see the look in another person's eyes that said they thought they were going to lose her was more than she could deal with. And to cry herself to sleep with another person in her mind who she couldn't bear the thought of never seeing again—that was what she was truly frightened of.

If the cancer came back.

Every day she lived with that. The worry that slowly ate at her brain and her thoughts like a termite gnawing on wood. She was a cancer survivor, she'd beaten the odds once, but there was always the chance that it could come back.

Since Ryan had stepped into her life in all his physical glory, she'd almost forgotten, almost felt normal for the first time in what seemed like forever. But then reality had come crashing down.

Her family would be heartbroken if she'd relapsed. No, they were already heartbroken that she'd gone through what she had. It would shatter their entire beings piece by piece if it had come back.

Jessica walked faster, moving as quickly as she could—as if doing so would make her heart heal. Or her mind forget the man she'd just walked out on last night. But the reality that confronted her was a sterile waiting room, and the smell of hospital that she'd grown to hate.

She should have brought someone with her. Bella. Her brother. Anyone. No matter how strong she tried to be, there was nothing worse than being alone.

Ryan felt like his head had been in a car crash. It was pounding, throbbing with a pain all of its own. He should have stopped to get a sling for his arm, too, but instead he'd swallowed a couple of pain relief pills he had in the car from the physio, and he was driving like a madman.

Bella had been a pain in the backside last night, refusing to tell him where he could find Jessica, but when he'd turned up at Steven's place this morning and told him the truth about how he felt, her brother had told him everything.

He was almost at the hospital.

Ryan had gotten over the fact that she'd written him a letter instead of telling him to his face. He'd gotten over the fact that she hadn't trusted him enough to tell him, to really let him in. He knew why she'd done it. He'd told her himself that he never wanted to see a loved one battle cancer, that he was scared of being truly heartbroken again, not knowing how much his words would have pierced her to the core. The last thing he wanted was to deal with her being sick, with anyone close facing something like cancer, but he certainly wasn't going to turn his back on Jessica. It wasn't her fault she'd been ill.

Once upon a time he'd thought he couldn't be strong enough to be there for someone again like he'd had to be there for his wife, but it didn't mean he wouldn't pull himself together for Jessica. Given the choice, he'd help her battle anything if it truly meant a future with her. Even just the chance at a future.

Maybe she was right not to have told him before. Maybe he would have run if he'd known about her cancer that first day he'd come back. To be honest, he probably would have avoided getting close to her at all, even via letters, had he known about her illness.

But this was *Jessica*. The woman he had now grown to love through letters and in person, who meant so much to him, that he couldn't be without her for however long they had together.

He pumped the accelerator a little harder, increasing his speed. If she told him to leave, he would. But he wasn't giving up without a fight. Without at least proving to her that he deserved a chance to be with her. To love her.

Jessica walked down the corridor. They wanted to keep her for a few hours, do some tests, and she needed to retrieve some things from the car. She knew how long these things could take, and she wanted to grab her book and sketch paper to draw on.

Heavy footsteps echoed out behind her but she didn't bother to turn. The hospital was full of noise, and even though she hated the place she felt safe here. So long as she didn't see too many cancer patients being pushed through the wards.

"Jessica!"

She stopped. Her feet actually stopped moving at the command, even though she didn't want them to. She squeezed her eyes shut for a nanosecond then started walking faster.

Ryan. She would know that voice anywhere and it was not one she wanted to hear. Not now. Maybe if she didn't turn around he'd figure it wasn't her. How had he found her anyway?

"Jessica!"

His voice was deep, strong, even more commanding this time.

She kept moving, head down. She wasn't going to let herself turn. Couldn't deal with him right now.

"Stop! Just stop."

The footfalls were right behind her. Running away wasn't an option. She had to stop. She forced her feet to a halt. Her shoulders heaved.

Why now? She didn't have the strength to deal with Ryan. Couldn't face him and see the hurt she knew she'd find there. The betrayal she knew he must be feeling. Why had he come?

"Jessica, look at me."

His voice was still commanding, but it was starting to crack.

"Look at me."

It was a whisper this time, barely audible. She still didn't move, not until his hand curled around her forearm and made her turn.

She could feel his big body behind her, so close all she wanted to do was lean back into him, to seek comfort from him.

But she couldn't. Not now. Not after what she'd done to him. If she'd just been honest from the beginning, instead of enjoying the fact that she could correspond with a friend who never asked her how she was coping, never reminded her of what she'd been through, she never would have had to face this kind of pain right now.

If she hadn't kept writing to him and pretending everything was normal, when she was actually in hospital and recovering...

Ryan's fingers traced up her arm, across her shoulder

and cupped her chin to make her turn properly. He gently tilted her face to look up at his.

Jessica opened her eyes, let him see her as the damaged, emotional mess she had become.

"Jessica, I love you."

His words almost made her crumple to the ground. No. He couldn't love her. Not after what she'd done, the way she'd deceived him, what she'd told him in her letter. He was saying it because he felt sorry for her, because he felt he had to care for her after what she'd been through.

The only thing worse than a man running out on you when you thought he loved you, was a man who was so honorable he felt he had to stay.

"Did you hear me?" Ryan's eyes flickered, searching her gaze. "I love you, Jessica."

She shook her head. "It's not enough." Her voice wobbled.

"Not enough?"

He stepped back, his hand leaving her skin to run through his hair. He looked like he was going to turn and storm off, like he didn't know what to do, but instead he propelled himself forward. She stepped back but he grabbed her, held her in place.

"I've been waiting for you my entire life, Jessica." His voice dropped as he reached both hands to her cheeks, holding her face. "It's like I've been living in slow motion, like my life has been building to this moment, like I've been waiting to meet you, to be with you, every day of my existence."

Tears started falling again, beating down her cheeks and curling into her mouth, their salty taste making it even harder to swallow. To say anything at all back to him.

She couldn't believe him.

"I don't want to hurt you." She stuttered the words out.

"Don't want to? Or are you afraid to let me in?"

She'd never seen him like this, so intense. One moment he looked broken, the next like the soldier he was. The powerful man she knew he must be when he was on duty. In uniform.

"I know what hurt is, Jessica." He stepped back again, like he needed distance from her to regain his strength. "I've seen men die, I've pulled triggers and thrown grenades and done plenty of things to hurt myself and others. I watched my wife die, in a hospital not unlike this, and I've had my heart break into so many pieces that I thought it would never heal."

Her tears ceased. She stood, arms hanging at her sides, face angled toward him. After pushing him away, and hoping he wouldn't come back, now she wanted to grab him and never let go.

"Despite everything I've already been through, do you know when I realized that I'd never truly known hurt before?" he asked.

She shook her head.

"When you told me in a letter you loved me, but then ran away from me. When I thought that maybe you might die, and I wouldn't be at your side to help fight it with you."

"Ryan."

"No." He put his hand up and started walking backward down the corridor as she followed him. "Don't pity me, or tell me you're sorry. Just don't."

He stopped when she did. Jessica wiped at her cheeks and took a deep breath. She'd tried to save him the pain of her problems and instead she'd done the opposite. His eyes were like the pathway to his soul. Big blue pools that blazed with hurt and betrayal. His skin was pale, so unlike its usual sun-tanned gold. Like all the blood had drained away.

There was only one thing she could tell him. And that was the truth. There was no point hiding behind her pride or her fear any longer. If he was prepared to put his own heart on the line, could honestly tell her that he felt for her so deeply that he'd face any battle with her, then she had to be honest with him in return.

If he was brave enough to deal with her cancer, then she owed it to him to face her own fears. To take a chance. To risk her own heart.

"I love you, too, Ryan." She only whispered but he'd heard her. Of course he'd heard her. "I'm sorry and I love you."

He didn't move. His feet were planted shoulder-width apart, like he was awaiting orders, and his face was frozen.

"Ryan?"

He blinked and looked back at her. "I think I fell in love with you before we even met."

Jessica started to cry again as she ran the distance between them. He opened his arms as she propelled herself forward, catching her as she landed against his chest. His hands circled her waist and hoisted her in the air, legs winding around his torso as she clung on to him like she'd never held anything in her life before.

The words from his letter, that last letter she'd found, played through her mind. It still seemed too good to be true, but she couldn't fight the way she felt any longer.

"I love you, Ryan. I love you so much it hurts."

Why hadn't she given him the chance to be here? To

hold her and protect her? Why had she not let it be his decision?

He pulled his face away from her neck, buried against her hair, to look at her. She leaned back in his arms, safe in his strong hold.

"Promise you'll never leave me again. Promise you'll never walk away again," he said urgently.

She nodded. "I promise."

Ryan watched her eyes, his now filled with tears, just like her own. He tipped her forward until their foreheads touched, before a big smile made his mouth twitch.

"We can fight anything together, Jessica. I promise."

She didn't have the chance to say it back. To tell him that she agreed. His lips searched for hers, his smooth skin whispering across hers as she clung on to him so hard her fingers dug into his shoulders. Ryan pulled her tighter against his body, one hand holding her, the other pressed into the back of her head as his lips continued their hungry assault on hers.

He was right. It was as if they'd been waiting their entire lives for one another.

And this was only just the beginning.

CHAPTER THIRTEEN

Dear Jessica,
Do you ever think about how your life turned
out? If you've made decisions, done things that
you should maybe have done differently? I often
wonder how it was I ended up here, whether I was
always destined to this life, even though I love
what I do. Maybe it's just my injury making me
think things like this, because I'm already sick of
being laid up and waiting for surgery.

Anyway, see you soon, okay? Maybe it's our
destiny to meet, or maybe I'm just getting carried
away. You decide.
Ryan

JESSICA LOOKED UP at Ryan as he cocooned her in his
arms. They were sitting on the grass as Hercules played
his duck-chasing game. She leaned back into Ryan, her
body fitting snugly between his legs so she could rest
on his chest.

"What are you thinking about?" Ryan asked, nuz-
zling her neck, his lips making goose pimples appear
on her skin.

"I'm wondering how neither of us realized that

we were writing love letters all this time," she said, smiling.

He wrapped his arms around her tighter. "Maybe we did and we just didn't want to admit it to ourselves."

She turned her body to face him, arms circling him as she sat between his legs still but pressing her chest to him now instead. She wrapped her legs around him, too.

"Have you told George about my cancer yet?"

Ryan dropped a kiss to her forehead. "Yeah."

She sat up straighter. "What did he say? What did you tell him?"

Ryan pulled her closer. "I haven't told him all the details yet, but I told him that you were in remission." He paused then sighed. "It was tough telling him, but he asked me a few questions and I did my best to answer honestly."

"Maybe I should say something to him. Talk to him about it."

Ryan shook his head. "No, I think *we* can talk about it as a couple with him. Make sure he understands how unlikely it is that it could come back, explain about the mastectomy, cover everything."

Jessica nodded.

"The last thing I want is for him to be scared of losing his future stepmom, too."

She snuggled into his shoulder, but Ryan pulled her back.

"What's wrong?"

Jessica squeezed her eyes shut before looking up at Ryan. Worry lines covered his face, brows pulled together.

"I'm scared about you going away again."

He closed his eyes as she tucked her face back into his neck.

"I have to go."

It sounded like the words were painful for him, like he didn't want to admit that he was going to be leaving her.

"I know, it's just…"

Ryan held her away from him and leaned back, his eyes searching hers. "I've got a lot to live for. Nothing's going to happen to me. I'm going to be back here before you know it, okay?"

She admired his bravery. "Okay."

"Your letters kept me alive on my last tour," he reminded her.

Jess laughed. "Yeah?"

"Yeah." Ryan pulled her back into him, his lips covering hers. "I'll be back here in a few months. Any sooner and you'd probably be sick of me."

Jessica just shook her head and pulled him closer. She doubted that could ever happen. "Just shut up and kiss me."

Ryan tipped her back onto the grass and pinned her down, hands above her head. He leaned over her, his shoulders blocking the sun from her eyes.

She giggled as he growled, his mouth moving closer to hers.

"You should know better than to give orders to a soldier."

Jessica sighed against his lips. If this was her punishment, she intended on ordering him around more often.

EPILOGUE

Dear Jessica,
I can't believe it's been six months since we were last together. Would you believe me if I said they were the longest six months of my life? Every day I think of you, not a day goes past when I don't think about what I have to come home to.

Not long ago, the word home *scared me. Now it makes me smile. Have I told you that you saved me? I know you'll say I saved myself, but you've made me whole. You gave me the strength to fight for what I believed in, what I wanted in my life, and somehow I managed to fight hard enough for you too.*

Before you ask, my arm is fine. But I'm not cut out for this any more. My heart's not in it, and for the first time in my life I'm looking forward to a desk job.

I promised you this would be my last tour, and I had the papers through today to confirm it. When you see me next, I'll be yours forever. I promise I'll never leave you again.

All my love, now and forever.
Ryan

* * *

JESSICA COULDN'T STAND still. She shifted her weight from foot to foot, gripping George's hand tight and grinning as he squeezed back.

"That kind of hurts."

She laughed. "Sorry. It's just…"

"I know."

Jessica watched as the first of the soldiers came through the gate. Her mouth was dry, heart hammering so loud she was struggling to hear herself think.

She had hated Ryan being away, but it had been good in a way. Jessica pulled George against her and his arm found her waist. He was as nervous and excited as she was. But he was also her friend. All these months with Ryan away had brought them closer, made them develop a bond that she knew would never be broken.

She couldn't wait to see the look on Ryan's face.

"Jess, do you…"

Suddenly she couldn't hear what George was saying. Her eyes were transfixed, body humming as she recognized the man walking through the gates and toward them.

Tousled dark hair, shorter than before he'd left, but unmistakably his. Tanned skin, broad shoulders, eyes that could find hers in any crowd.

Ryan.

She knew George had left her side, that he'd already seen his dad. But she was powerless to move. She didn't know whether to leap in the air and squeal with excitement or cry her eyes out that he was actually here. Alive. Whole.

She drunk in the sight of him in his combat uniform. Camouflage pants and shirt, the same uniform she'd seen hanging in his closet that day. He looked good enough to eat and he was almost standing in front of her now, his son by his side.

"Hey, baby," he said.

She couldn't move. Words stuck in her throat.

But he didn't care. His smile lit up his entire face as he dropped his bag and grabbed her around the waist, swinging her up in the air and kissing her so hard she almost lost her breath.

"Ryan…" His name came out a whisper, like she couldn't truly believe he was back.

He kissed her again, his lips soft against hers this time, like he was whispering back to her. He only pulled away to put his other arm around his son.

"I've been waiting for this day for six months, and I'm never leaving either of you again. Okay?"

George nodded and all Jessica could do was grin up at him, feeling giddy with the sight of him before her, with the strength of him beneath her touch.

"Welcome home, Dad."

She reached for George and the three of them hugged, snuggled up close together.

"I'm so lucky to have you guys as my family." Jessica almost choked on her words but she had to say them. She *was* lucky. To have a man like Ryan by her side and a boy like George in her life.

"We're the lucky ones, right, bud?" Ryan asked his son.

George laughed and stepped back, quickly rubbing at his face to hide his tears.

But Jessica knew better. She was the lucky one.

She'd fought cancer, she'd faced heartache and loss, and yet she'd still managed to find Ryan. He'd made everything right again.

Today was like the start of their new life together.

He'd returned home safely from war. She'd passed all her tests with flying colors. And George had finally accepted her like they'd known one another all their lives.

"Shall we go home?" she asked.

Ryan laughed and George nudged him in the side.

"You got it?" Ryan asked his son.

George blocked Jessica and gave his father something from his pocket.

"What's going on?" she asked curiously.

Ryan passed his son his kit bag and they grinned at one another, before he turned to face her, reaching for one of her hands.

"This time when I was away, I wrote to George, too, as often as I wrote to you."

Jessica nodded. She knew that already.

"So that's how I knew all your tests had gone fine, and that George was coping okay. That he wasn't scared of losing you, too, now that the two of you had become so close."

She wasn't sure where this was going. "I know, Ryan. George and I talk about everything, we don't have any secrets."

George laughed.

She turned to glare at his cheeky response but he just shrugged.

"There is something he's been keeping secret." He paused. "In one of my last letters, I asked George a question." Ryan smiled over at his son again, before dropping to one knee.

Suddenly the noise of the airport, the hustle and bustle around them, disappeared. She could hardly see straight, could only focus on Ryan on one knee before her. Surely not?

Her heart started to thump. Hard.

"I know it's tradition to ask the bride's family for permission first, but in this case I thought it was George's permission we needed."

Oh, my. Her mouth was dry, she couldn't move. Bride? Had she heard him right?

"Jessica, will you do me the honor of becoming my wife? Of becoming George's stepmum?" Ryan asked huskily.

Jessica couldn't help the excited squeal as it left her lips. "Yes!" She grinned as Ryan rose. "Yes, yes, yes."

He leaned in and kissed her, touching his nose to hers, his forehead pressed against hers.

"Are you sure?" he whispered.

"I've never been more sure of anything in my life."

Ryan stepped back and held up her left hand, opening his other palm to reveal a ring. She watched as he raised it and placed it on her finger. A single solitaire on a platinum band.

"I can't believe you were in on this." Jessica turned to George, who was blushing from ear to ear. He just shrugged, obviously thrilled to have surprised her.

Jess turned her attention back to the ring, holding it up to the light to watch it sparkle.

"Do you like it?" Ryan asked anxiously.

She reached for him and held him tight, never wanting to let him go. "I love it."

He kissed her on the top of her head and took her hand.

"Let's go home, family."

Jessica reached for George's hand with her free one as they walked from the airport.

Home had never sounded so good.

0611 Gen Std HB

JULY 2011
HARDBACK TITLES

ROMANCE

The Marriage Betrayal	Lynne Graham
The Ice Prince	Sandra Marton
Doukakis's Apprentice	Sarah Morgan
Surrender to the Past	Carole Mortimer
Heart of the Desert	Carol Marinelli
Reckless Night in Rio	Jennie Lucas
Her Impossible Boss	Cathy Williams
The Replacement Wife	Caitlin Crews
Dating and Other Dangers	Natalie Anderson
The S Before Ex	Mira Lyn Kelly
Her Outback Commander	Margaret Way
A Kiss to Seal the Deal	Nikki Logan
Baby on the Ranch	Susan Meier
The Army Ranger's Return	Soraya Lane
Girl in a Vintage Dress	Nicola Marsh
Rapunzel in New York	Nikki Logan
The Doctor & the Runaway Heiress	Marion Lennox
The Surgeon She Never Forgot	Melanie Milburne

HISTORICAL

Seduced by the Scoundrel	Louise Allen
Unmasking the Duke's Mistress	Margaret McPhee
To Catch a Husband…	Sarah Mallory
The Highlander's Redemption	Marguerite Kaye

MEDICAL™

The Playboy of Harley Street	Anne Fraser
Doctor on the Red Carpet	Anne Fraser
Just One Last Night...	Amy Andrews
Suddenly Single Sophie	Leonie Knight

JULY 2011
LARGE PRINT TITLES

ROMANCE

A Stormy Spanish Summer	Penny Jordan
Taming the Last St Claire	Carole Mortimer
Not a Marrying Man	Miranda Lee
The Far Side of Paradise	Robyn Donald
The Baby Swap Miracle	Caroline Anderson
Expecting Royal Twins!	Melissa McClone
To Dance with a Prince	Cara Colter
Molly Cooper's Dream Date	Barbara Hannay

HISTORICAL

Lady Folbroke's Delicious Deception	Christine Merrill
Breaking the Governess's Rules	Michelle Styles
Her Dark and Dangerous Lord	Anne Herries
How To Marry a Rake	Deb Marlowe

MEDICAL™

Sheikh, Children's Doctor...Husband	Meredith Webber
Six-Week Marriage Miracle	Jessica Matthews
Rescued by the Dreamy Doc	Amy Andrews
Navy Officer to Family Man	Emily Forbes
St Piran's: Italian Surgeon, Forbidden Bride	Margaret McDonagh
The Baby Who Stole the Doctor's Heart	Dianne Drake

AUGUST 2011
HARDBACK TITLES

ROMANCE

Bride for Real	Lynne Graham
From Dirt to Diamonds	Julia James
The Thorn in His Side	Kim Lawrence
Fiancée for One Night	Trish Morey
The Untamed Argentinian	Susan Stephens
After the Greek Affair	Chantelle Shaw
The Highest Price to Pay	Maisey Yates
Under the Brazilian Sun	Catherine George
There's Something About a Rebel...	Anne Oliver
The Crown Affair	Lucy King
Australia's Maverick Millionaire	Margaret Way
Rescued by the Brooding Tycoon	Lucy Gordon
Not-So-Perfect Princess	Melissa McClone
The Heart of a Hero	Barbara Wallace
Swept Off Her Stilettos	Fiona Harper
Mr Right There All Along	Jackie Braun
The Tortured Rebel	Alison Roberts
Dating Dr Delicious	Laura Iding

HISTORICAL

Married to a Stranger	Louise Allen
A Dark and Brooding Gentleman	Margaret McPhee
Seducing Miss Lockwood	Helen Dickson
The Highlander's Return	Marguerite Kaye

MEDICAL™

The Doctor's Reason to Stay	Dianne Drake
Career Girl in the Country	Fiona Lowe
Wedding on the Baby Ward	Lucy Clark
Special Care Baby Miracle	Lucy Clark

AUGUST 2011
LARGE PRINT TITLES

ROMANCE

Jess's Promise	Lynne Graham
Not For Sale	Sandra Marton
After Their Vows	Michelle Reid
A Spanish Awakening	Kim Lawrence
In the Australian Billionaire's Arms	Margaret Way
Abby and the Bachelor Cop	Marion Lennox
Misty and the Single Dad	Marion Lennox
Daycare Mum to Wife	Jennie Adams

HISTORICAL

Miss in a Man's World	Anne Ashley
Captain Corcoran's Hoyden Bride	Annie Burrows
His Counterfeit Condesa	Joanna Fulford
Rebellious Rake, Innocent Governess	Elizabeth Beacon

MEDICAL™

Cedar Bluff's Most Eligible Bachelor	Laura Iding
Doctor: Diamond in the Rough	Lucy Clark
Becoming Dr Bellini's Bride	Joanna Neil
Midwife, Mother...Italian's Wife	Fiona McArthur
St Piran's: Daredevil, Doctor...Dad!	Anne Fraser
Single Dad's Triple Trouble	Fiona Lowe